Tomorrow's
PROMISE

Tomorrow's
PROMISE

JUDY BAER

Scripture Union
130 City Road London EC1V 2NJ

First published in the USA by Bethany House Publishers,
6820 Auto Club Road,
Minneapolis, Minnesota 55438

First published in the UK by Scripture Union, 1992

ISBN 0 86201 791 2

British Library Cataloguing-in-Publication Data.
A catalogue record for this book is available
from the British Library.

All scripture quotations in this publication are from the
Holy Bible, New International Version. Copyright 1973,
1978, 1984, International Bible Society.
Published by Hodder and Stoughton.

Phototypeset by Falcon Typographic Art Ltd, Fife, Scotland
Printed and bound in Great Britain by
Cox and Wyman Ltd, Reading

For Donna,
who helps me
keep it together

Lexi sat in her father's easy chair, dangling her slender legs over the arms, silently watching.

In the middle of the room was a card table and four chairs. Lexi's little brother Ben knelt on one of the chairs, his arms propped on the table, his chin cupped in his hand. He stared intently at the puzzle pieces spread across the table.

Lexi's grandmother, Grace Carson, also stared at the puzzle pieces on the table. Her eyes were vague and unfocused.

'The piece you've got goes here, Grandma,' Ben announced. With gentle fingers he guided his grandmother's hand to an open space in the nearly completed puzzle. 'You're doing well, Grandma,' Ben encouraged. 'Look, we're almost done.'

The puzzle was simple, with large pieces and bright

colours depicting cartoon animals. Ben had put the puzzle together a dozen times. He never tired of it.

'Where does this go, Ben?' Grandma asked, staring blankly at the puzzle piece she'd picked up.

'It's the elephant's trunk, Grandma. It goes here.' Ben pointed to the spot with a stubby finger.

Lexi held back a sigh. Her little brother, who suffered from Down's syndrome, was more adept and less confused than her grandmother. Ben gently directed Grandmother's hand over the puzzle again and helped her fit the piece into its place.

Lexi watched them sadly, thinking of the ways her grandmother had changed.

Grandmother suffered from Alzheimer's disease, a deterioration of the brain which leads to disorientation and forgetfulness. The disease seemed to be drawing her deeper and deeper into confusion.

It had been difficult for Ben, with his own limited capabilities, to understand why an adult would behave in such a child-like manner. He was often frightened by Grandma's strange behaviour. Since Grandmother had come to live with the Leightons after her husband's death, there had been many sleepless nights.

In the past few weeks, Ben had finally come to understand that Grandmother's illness would not go away. As he began to realise that Grandmother needed his help, he began to feel important in her life. Often, as he was doing today, he would care for her in his own simple way, getting her glasses of water, helping her to walk down the hall, feeding her bites of his own snacks or guiding her hand across a puzzle that had grown too complicated for her to understand. Ben was pleased to be 'helping' Grandma.

Lexi gazed at Ben with admiration. She wasn't nearly so proud of her own response to Grandmother's illness. Lexi felt a blush creep over her cheeks as she thought of how she had behaved when Grandma Carson had first come to live with them.

At first Lexi had been overwhelmed by the sadness she felt. Grandpa Carson was dead, and Grandmother's personality was so changed that Lexi hardly knew her. Instead of the efficient, loving grandmother she'd always known, Grandma Carson was a confused ineffective shadow of her former self.

Lexi's sadness had turned to frustration as Grandmother persisted in her bizarre behaviour – talking to herself in mirrors or becoming lost in the house and wandering onto the front lawn.

As Grandmother's condition worsened, her behaviour became even more unpredictable. Lexi had felt an overwhelming sense of embarrassment. It became too painful and risky for Lexi to have her friends come to her home. They might see her grandmother walking around the house with her clothes on backwards, muttering to herself. Grandmother wasn't normal any more.

One day, Lexi had taken Grandmother to the chemist's where she had shoplifted some chewing gum beside the cash register.

The past weeks had been the most painful time in Lexi's life.

Unfortunately, Lexi had struggled through them

alone. Her parents were too caught up in the maze of Grandmother's illness to attend to her special emotional needs at this time.

Todd Winston, Lexi's boyfriend, had been unable to comprehend the depth of Lexi's frustration. He'd accused her of being impatient and unkind to her grandmother, when in reality, Lexi felt she was doing everything within her power to be both patient and kind.

'Where are Mum and Dad?' Ben asked, interrupting Lexi's thoughts.

'In the kitchen.' She could hear her parents' quiet conversation as they bent over the kitchen table. They were talking about Grandmother – as usual. Every night after supper, Jim and Marilyn Leighton struggled over the question of what to do with Grandma Carson.

Grandmother was becoming more and more difficult to care for at home. Yet Lexi's mother resisted sending her to a nursing home. Lexi laid her head back on the chair and stared at the ceiling. She wondered how long her parents would spend discussing the same thing night after night.

She detected a rise in her parents' voices – an almost sure signal they were disagreeing on something.

In the living room, Grandmother was making odd sounds as she continued to finger the puzzle pieces. Only Ben seemed happy and content as he worked the brightly coloured puzzle again, humming to himself.

Lexi squeezed her eyes tightly shut, wishing she could blank out these moments in her life as easily as she could close out the light in the room. Then she swung her feet to the floor. Her elbows on her knees, she buried her face in her hands.

Gone. Everything's gone. Grandpa's dead. Grandma's mind is confused, disoriented, suffering. And Todd – is he gone too? Lexi recalled the arguments they'd had, the ugly way they'd parted.

He'd called her a *hypocrite* and accused her of being *unkind* and *impatient* with Grandmother.

Perhaps at the beginning of Grandma's illness that might have been true. But with God's help, Lexi had struggled to overcome those road-blocks in her life. She'd had to fight to hang on to her faith. Through it all, she'd learned that God was with her, carrying her, supporting her, urging her forward. That knowledge was the stabilising quality in her unpredictable life right now.

Lexi heard her father leave the house, and she rose to join her mother in the kitchen. Mrs Leighton looked at her daughter with sad, compassionate eyes. Her mother was so much thinner now. Her care of Grandma had taken its physical toll on her body.

She took Lexi's hand in her own. 'What's wrong, love?'

Lexi felt a rush of tears well in her throat, but she didn't speak. She couldn't tell her mother how she was feeling. Mrs Leighton had to be feeling much, much worse. After all, Grandma Carson was her mother.

Mrs Leighton was resting her elbows on the kitchen table. She cupped her chin in her hands and stared thoughtfully out of the window. 'I must have been a difficult child to raise,' she said.

What was her mother talking about?

'I had allergies, you know,' Mrs Leighton continued. 'I couldn't drink milk or eat anything with wheat flour in it. I broke out in hives if I ate strawberries.'

'You don't have those allergies now, Mum,' Lexi pointed out.

'No. I expect I outgrew them,' Mrs Leighton explained. 'But when I was small I was a very picky eater – a fussy child. Dad used to walk me at night to get me to sleep. Sometimes either he or Mum would rub my back or sing to me for an hour or more before I'd finally settle down. Thankfully, when I got older, the allergies seemed to be less of a problem. That's when mother started teaching me to sew.'

'How old were you?'

'I wasn't more than eight or nine when I first picked up a needle and thread.'

Lexi liked to sew her own clothes, too. She'd learned from her mother. Now she was hearing for the first time that it was a legacy from Grandma Carson.

'I must have made a dozen pot-holders that first summer I started to sew,' Mrs Leighton chuckled. 'I gave the nice ones to relatives for Christmas, and Mum kept all the lopsided ones. She said they were the most special. When we were home for Dad's funeral, I found those pot-holders in her drawer. She was still using them!' Mrs Leighton's eyes brightened at the thought. 'Did I ever tell you about the time I attempted to sew a party dress?'

Lexi shook her head.

'I don't know what came over me.' She threw her head back and laughed lightly. 'I saw a beautiful taffeta dress with a full skirt and a low cut neck in a magazine. I decided that was the dress for me. I hadn't done too much fancy sewing at that point, but I was determined to make that dress. I nagged my mother for two weeks before she took me to town and bought the most wonderful blue taffeta. I can still feel that fabric, Lexi. It was so luxurious.'

'Do you still have the dress?' Lexi asked eagerly.

'Oh, no. It never did become a dress.'

'Why?' Lexi leaned forward, her curiosity.

'Because I thought I knew everything about sewing, and I assumed I could sew that dress without my mother's help.

'One afternoon, when Mother was at the church, I spread the taffeta on the dining room table, laid the pattern pieces on top and started to cut.'

'And?'

'Well, I didn't know as much about sewing as I thought I did. I laid the pattern pieces on the fabric any way I could. I didn't bother to read the instructions. You can imagine that didn't work very well.'

Lexi knew from her own sewing experience that her mother's mistake was a disastrous one. 'What happened then?'

'It might not have been so bad if that had been my only mistake. But I eagerly cut off all the notches that show where to match the pieces together, cutting off the seam allowance as well.'

'Oh, oh,' Lexi clapped her hand over her mouth.

'And I didn't mark the darts either.' Mrs Leighton started to chuckle. 'By the time I finished the dress, it looked as if it had been put together by a committee. And of course it was far too small.'

'Oh, Mum. I'm sorry!'

'Don't be. It wasn't so bad, really. My mother forgave me for my childish haste. She made the best out of a bad situation. We took the dress apart, laid it out again and made doll clothes for all my cousins.' Mrs Leighton's eyes twinkled. 'They were much happier getting those for Christmas than pot-holders!'

'Grandma didn't get mad with you for ruining all that fabric?' Lexi asked.

'Oh no. She just shook her head and never said another word about it after the doll clothes were done. I learned more from that experience and her silence than if she'd given me a lecture about wastefulness and attempting to do things without direction and help.'

'Grandma was pretty smart,' Lexi commented.

'Your grandmother was one of the smartest women I've ever known, Lexi.' Mrs Leighton's eyes filled with tears. 'That's why it's so difficult to see her deteriorating a little bit every day. She's losing the best part of herself. Her mind.'

'I hate this disease,' Lexi said with a vengeance. 'I hate it. I hate it. I hate it!' Mrs Leighton laid her hand on Lexi's arm. 'I do too, love. We have to do now what Grandma did for me. We have to make the best of a bad situation.'

'I know that it's my turn to do something for

Grandma. Every day I pray that we'll make it through the next twenty-four hours without any major problems.'

Mrs Leighton's look was pained. 'I know it's terribly hard on you and Ben having Grandmother disrupting your lives like this, but I feel that we should care for her as long as we can.'

Mrs Leighton sighed, running her fingers through her hair. 'It's tough to know what's right. I have people telling me that she's too much responsibility, that a nursing home is the best place for her. Then, I think of all the time and love that she gave to me. I want to give just a little of that back. Can you understand that, Lexi? I pray every day that you'll understand.'

'How do you keep your faith in God, Mum?' Lexi wondered. 'Isn't it hard to believe at all after seeing Grandma this way?' Lexi knew how difficult her own daily struggle had become. It was particularly hard now that she didn't have Todd to confide in.

'When we have faith in God, Lexi, we have something that the devil doesn't want us to have. He's our adversary and wants to bring that faith of ours to an end. He wants our faith to be weak, not strong. When things are difficult, I remind myself that the devil thrives on our bad times. He wants us to doubt ourselves and our faith in God. I try not to give in to self-pity or anger because then he's getting exactly what he wants from us.'

Her mother's look was determined. 'I have to ask God for help to do this though, Lexi, because I know I can't do it on my own. All our faith and strength for everything that happens to us each day comes from God. When things are going well and we're happy, we tend to forget this. We think we've got a handle on our lives. But when things whirl out of control, we realise again how helpless we are without our Heavenly Father.'

Mrs Leighton reached across the table and patted Lexi's hands. 'What all this boils down to is that I want you to know that I really care about you and what you're going through. I worry sometimes that I've got so caught up in caring for my mother that I've forgotten how it's affecting you children.

'I want you to say whatever you really feel, Lexi. If you're angry, guilty or frustrated, say it. Don't keep it inside.'

'I don't like to be negative about it, Mum. I know it's hard enough as it is for you without worrying about me.'

'I always have time for you, Lexi. Always.'

Lexi looked at her mother with understanding. 'I know you always have had time, Mum, but lately Grandma takes all your attention.'

Lexi was silent then. It hadn't been easy sharing her parents with her grandmother.

'I think it's perfectly normal,' Mrs Leighton agreed, 'to feel that there is no time for you. But you have to ask, Lexi. You have to let Dad and me know when you need us.'

'But I feel awful, Mum. Every time I need to talk to you I feel as if I'm taking you away from Grandma. And if I feel the least bit jealous of the time you spend with Grandma, then I feel terrible, because Grandma's so helpless.' Lexi looked down at the floor. It was hard to tell her mother these things.

'Yesterday Grandma must have asked me a dozen times where you were. Every time I told her you were in the kitchen, she'd just nod her head, then ask me again. I felt like yelling at her, Mum.' Lexi's eyes filled with tears. 'I felt so awful. I know she can't help it that she doesn't remember.'

'This is an ugly disease, Lexi,' her mother said matter-of-factly. 'When one person is ill, the effects of it naturally spread throughout the entire family.' Mrs Leighton looked sad again. 'Poor Ben. He asked me the other day if he was going to catch Grandma's disease. I think he was afraid he was going to forget how to tie his shoes and get dressed in the morning!'

By now both of them had tears in their eyes as Lexi's mother went on about their mutual problems.

'Ben's fears are very real. I tried to assure him that Alzheimer's wasn't catchy, even though it's ended up affecting our entire family. I just hope he understood.'

'Maybe I can talk to him later today,' Lexi offered.

'Thanks, love.' Mrs Leighton's expression was serious. 'Lexi, there's one other thing I have to ask of you.'

'What's that, Mum?'

'I've been noticing that you've been staying at home far too much. I haven't seen any of your friends over here for ages. When Binky and Jennifer call, you talk to them for a few minutes and then hang up. I think that's wrong, Lexi. You need to spend more time with your friends.'

'But Grandma –'

'What would be best for Grandma – for all of us – would be for you to go on with your own life, Lexi. Don't let her presence here stop you from living normally.'

'It's not that easy, Mum.' It was difficult to explain to her mother about the embarrassment and pity she felt at the thought of exposing her grandmother's condition to anyone outside the family. She couldn't bear to have her friends remember her beloved grandmother as she was today. She wished that Todd, Jennifer and Binky could have known her grandmother as Lexi knew her. As the loving, funny and kind person she had been.

Suddenly an argument broke out between Ben and Grandma in the living room.

'No, you can't do that. It doesn't go there. No. No. No!'

'But Grandma, that's where it belongs,' Ben wailed.

'You took my puzzle piece,' Grandma said angrily, pointing a finger at Ben. She and Ben tugged at the single puzzle piece.

'I can show you where it goes, Grandma,' Ben said sweetly. 'That's the dog's nose. See?'

Grandma shook her head stubbornly, refusing to be convinced.

'Oh dear.' Mrs Leighton entered the room. 'Ben, why don't you let Grandma try the puzzle piece someplace else? Then you can put the doggy's nose where it belongs?'

Ben's lower lip came out in a pout. 'I know where

it goes and she won't believe me. It's no fun doing puzzles with Grandma,' he said as a large tear rolled down his cheek. 'She won't share. She's not nice any more.'

Grandma, through the cloud of confusion that surrounded her, seemed to understand Ben's final statement. She broke into tears.

Ben, sensing that he'd caused his grandma's unhappiness, began to wail.

Lexi had entered the room also, and stood against the door-frame with her eyes closed. A blackness seemed to descend over her as she closed out the distressing sounds around her. She imagined her life to be moving along a long dark tunnel. There was no light at the end of it.

~ 2 ~

Lexi jumped out of bed at the first sound of her alarm clock.

Hurrying through her shower, she dressed in record time. She glided down the stairs and grabbed a piece of toast from the table. 'Hello, everyone. And goodbye.' She smiled at her parents as they sat drinking their morning coffee. 'Must go. I'm late for school.'

'Late?' Mr Leighton questioned, 'It's only –'

'I want to be there early today,' Lexi explained as she opened the door. 'See you after school. Bye.' She hurried down the path with a purposeful step. It wasn't until she was out of sight of her own house that her walk slowed and she gave a quick sigh of relief.

She'd done it. She'd got out of the house without

having some sort of emotional encounter with her grandmother.

Lexi felt sick inside at the notion that she was avoiding her own grandmother, but she knew it was true. The emotional roller coaster that Grandmother put her on was more than she could bear today. It was too difficult to concentrate in school when she thought about what was going on at home.

'Hey, Lexi, wait,' a familiar voice called. Lexi turned around to see Jennifer Golden hurrying towards her. 'You're out of the house earlier than usual,' Jennifer observed. Her blonde hair danced like a halo around her head, and she was chewing gum vigorously as she talked.

'I have so much homework I can hardly carry my backpack,' Jennifer complained. 'Are they spreading it on really thick because school is almost over for the summer or what?'

Lexi nodded sympathetically, 'I've had a lot of homework too. I think it's some sort of teachers' plot they hatched up in the staff room.'

'No doubt about it,' Jennifer said agreeably. They walked together in silence for a few moments before Jennifer glanced at Lexi out of the corner of her eye. 'How's your grandmother?'

Lexi wrinkled her nose. 'Okay, I guess. About the same.'

'I take it you don't want to talk about it,' Jennifer replied.

Lexi nodded, feeling a wave of guilt wash over her. She couldn't win! She didn't want to be mean to Grandmother by ignoring her or refusing to talk about her to her friends, yet she really didn't want to talk about it. It was just too painful.

Jennifer didn't press the issue. Instead, she brought up one equally painful. 'Have you seen Todd lately?'

Lexi didn't want to talk about Todd either. 'Not lately,' Lexi said flatly, hoping that Jennifer would get the idea and change the topic of conversation.

But Jennifer didn't. 'What's going on between you two?' she asked. 'I don't get it. You're perfect for each other and as far as I can tell, you're hardly speaking.'

'I haven't had time for anyone lately,' Lexi pointed out.

'Todd hasn't sat with us at lunch for nearly a week,' Jennifer said. 'He's been sitting with a bunch of fellows from the Emerald Tones.' She looked at Lexi suspiciously. 'He's never done that before. Not until now.'

Lexi felt Jennifer's accusing stare burn through her. She gave a defeated shrug. 'All right. We had an argument.'

'You and Todd? Arguing? I don't believe it.'

'Well, believe it,' Lexi said bluntly. 'I don't know if Todd and I will ever speak to one another again.'

Jennifer's blue eyes grew huge with astonishment. 'You broke up?'

'I guess you could call it that,' Lexi muttered.

'So that's what it's all about.'

'All what's about?' Lexi wondered.

'It's why I haven't seen Todd smile all week. It's why he stamps around the hall like there's a cloud

22

over his head. He shoots out of the parking lot after school without talking to Harry or Egg either.'

Lexi shrugged. 'I don't know about any of that.'

'You two seemed so perfect for each other,' Jennifer wailed. 'I can't believe you had a fight.' She pressed Lexi with her gaze. 'What was it about?'

'It's too hard to explain, Jennifer.'

'What do you mean? I'm your best friend. You can tell me. What did you fight about?'

'I don't want to talk about it, Jennifer,' Lexi pleaded. 'It's just too ugly.'

Jennifer might have persisted if tears had not welled up in Lexi's eyes.

'All right, all right. I suppose this isn't the best place to discuss this,' Jennifer admitted. 'But you need to talk to someone, Lexi Leighton. I'm one of your best friends. I'm here for you. I want you to know that.'

Lexi nodded mutely. She would talk all day and all night if she thought it would help her relationship with Todd, but she didn't believe that was possible.

He wasn't yet able to understand the strain of living with someone with Alzheimer's. He couldn't understand how Grandmother's deteriorating mind forced the family to treat her like a child. Their whole fight had been a series of dreadful misunderstandings.

It reminded Lexi of the time her mother had asked her to untangle a knot of gold chains in her jewellery box. The more Lexi had tried to untangle the chains, the tighter the knots had become. It was hard to imagine she would ever be able to untangle them.

It was like that with her and Todd. She didn't

know how to fix things without making them much, much worse.

Egg met Jennifer and Lexi at the front door of the school. 'There you are,' Egg said, pointing at Lexi. 'I'm glad you came early today.'

'What's up, Egg-O?' Lexi said, sounding more cheerful than she felt.

'I've got an assignment for you for the *River Review*.' Egg waved a slip of paper in his hand. 'Mrs Drummond wants you and Todd to take pictures of the speech and debate teams this morning. Pronto. Fast as you can.'

'This morning? Todd and I?' Lexi echoed.

'You heard it. Apparently they weren't on the list last time you were taking pictures. She wants them right away. All the teams are meeting in the speech room at nine o'clock. Todd's already there setting up. Here's your excuse from class.' He thrust the slip of paper into Lexi's hand. 'It shouldn't take more than an hour to get everything done.'

Terrific, Lexi thought as she stuffed books into her locker. Just what she needed this morning. She'd got out of the house without having to confront Grandmother, only to have to endure a third degree from Jennifer. And now this!

She and Todd hadn't spoken since the afternoon of their disagreement at her house.

The photo session was as awkward as Lexi had feared it might be. Mrs Drummond had asked Egg to help Lexi and Todd set up the photos. Egg spent most of his time staring from Todd to Lexi and back again, completely confused by their silence toward each other. It wasn't until the last team was being shot that the icy tension in the room began to crackle.

'I think Mike and Ted should stand up and Mary Ann and Susie should sit down,' Todd announced as Egg was arranging the foursome.

'I think the girls should stand up and the guys should sit down,' Lexi interrupted.

'That's not the way we did the others,' Todd said.

'So it's time for a change,' Lexi retorted.

'But we've always done it this way,' Todd protested.

Lexi glared at him, 'Does everything always have to be done your way? The way things have *always* been done? You know, Todd, sometimes you don't see the whole picture. You just see part of it.' Lexi was really referring to the situation with Grandma, but she couldn't help herself.

Todd glared at her. 'I'm seeing the whole picture. It's just four people from the speech team.'

'This picture is going to appear in the *River Review* and probably in the yearbook. Isn't it going to look a little strange if every single one of the teams is posed exactly the same way? People aren't all the same, Todd. They shouldn't be treated that way.'

Egg's head swivelled back and forth as if it were on an oiled ball bearing. The members of the speech team looked incredulous.

'Just take the picture,' Egg roared. 'I don't know what you two are arguing about, but I don't think it's the way the group is posed.'

Lexi and Todd both cast ashamed glances towards the floor. Without comment, Todd snapped the final pictures. Once the speech team members had escaped, Egg turned to them. He balled his hands into fists and placed them on his scrawny hips, his legs straddled, his eyes flaring.

'Now what was *that* all about?' he demanded.

'Todd wanted the boys to stand in the back and I wanted the girls to stand in the back,' Lexi pointed out. 'That's all.'

'It had nothing to do with that pose.' Egg's eyes narrowed. 'I heard all that business about not understanding the "whole picture." Do you two want to tell me what's going on?'

Lexi glanced at the big pendulum clock on the wall and shook her head. 'Sorry, I've got to get to another class. I'd love to stay and chat, but I really can't.' She picked up her camera bag and her backpack and hurried for the door.

Halfway down the hall, she heard galloping footsteps behind her. She sighed and slowed down. Without turning around, she closed her eyes and said, 'Hello, Egg. What do you want?'

Egg skidded to a stop as he caught up with her. 'I want you to talk to me, Lexi,' he said. His eyes were full of concern and caring. 'I've never seen either of you behave like that. You've never been in a hurry to leave Todd before. And Todd gritted his teeth and packed his camera bag without saying another word to me.'

Lexi nodded. 'I'm sorry, Egg. I know I was mean.'

'He's hurting, Lexi. He really is. And he's upset.'

'Todd's upset?' Lexi echoed. 'Well, I'm upset too, Egg.'

Egg grimaced, 'Listen, I normally don't like to get in the middle of things, but you need to know that Todd is really crazy about you. He misses you terribly. I've been trying to get Todd to tell me what happened between you and he won't say anything.'

'Nothing?'

'Well, he did say something weird. He said he didn't understand you.' Egg shrugged his shoulders. 'I don't know why that should upset him. I've never understood women. Any of them – not even my sister. And I live with her.'

'Let's just say that we've had a misunderstanding that can't be resolved right now.' Lexi laid a hand on Egg's arm. 'Thanks for caring, but I think this is something that isn't going to work itself out.'

Egg's eyes looked pained. 'I thought you two could handle anything.'

Lexi could see the disappointment and the confusion in his face, and it hurt her deeply.

Egg turned to her. 'Are you sure you can't work this out, Lexi? You and Todd belong together.'

His words echoed through her brain all day long. She managed to escape a few minutes early from school so that she could avoid Jennifer and Binky. She wanted to walk home alone. There was so much to think about.

At one time Lexi had believed that she could work anything out. She'd felt strong, confident and sure of herself. But that was before her grandfather had died and her grandmother became so ill. She felt different too after Todd's accusation that she was a hypocrite.

After much spiritual struggle, Lexi had come to discover what God and her faith actually meant to her. The strength she'd gained from that knowledge had carried her through Grandmother's difficult times and through her break-up with Todd. Ironically, having learned so much about herself and her faith, Lexi felt less in control of her life than ever. She'd been forced to lean on God for strength while the world around her collapsed.

Lexi noticed her grandmother in the window as she neared her house. When she went in, she saw that she was reading her Bible. The sight surprised her. On good days, Grandma did read, though Lexi hadn't seen her pick up a book for several days.

Grandmother looked over the top of her wire-rimmed glasses and smiled. 'Hello, Lexi,' she said, her voice strong and steady.

Lexi knew immediately that Grandmother's mind was clear today. That was the awful part about Alzheimer's, Lexi thought. She could be clear and rational one moment and confused the next. Lexi was learning to enjoy every good moment her grandmother had.

'Hello, Grandmother,' Lexi said. 'You're looking well today.'

'I've been reading.' Grandmother gently patted her Bible.

Lexi dropped her schoolbag on the chair and sat on the floor by Grandmother's feet. She curled up and leaned her head on her knee. Grandmother seemed content, and ran her fingers through Lexi's hair. Her gentleness soothed away the tension of the day. Lexi felt her shoulders relaxing. It felt so good to be here. So natural. Lexi realised how much she'd missed this attention.

'What a wonderful afternoon it's been,' Grandma said with genuine pleasure.

'Oh?' Lexi murmured.

'Yes. I've been reading the Scriptures and it's been such a comfort to me. Now you've come home and I can spend time with my dear granddaughter. Those are two very special pleasures to me.'

Lexi smiled up at her. 'What have you been reading, Grandma?'

'It's my favourite passage in all the Bible,' Grandma said with a smile. 'The Twenty-third Psalm,' In her soft, wavering voice, Grandmother began to read:

The Lord is my shepherd, I shall lack nothing. He makes me lie down in green pastures, he leads me beside quiet waters, he restores my soul. He guides me in paths of righteousness for his name's sake. Even though I walk through the valley of the shadow of death, I will fear no evil, for you are with me; your rod and staff, they comfort me. You prepare a table before me in the presence of my enemies. You anoint my head with oil; my cup overflows. Surely goodness and love will follow me all the days of my life, and I will dwell in the house of the Lord forever.

'That's good,' Lexi mused. 'I like that passage too.'

Grandma pointed her gnarled finger at the passage. 'I particularly like this part:

Even though I walk through the valley of the shadow of death, I will fear no evil, for you are with me; your rod and staff, they comfort me.

'Do you know why, Lexi?'

'Because God promises to be with you?' Lexi asked.

'More than that. This passage could be frightening because it says, "Even though I walk through *the valley of the shadow of death*, I fear no evil." The valley of the shadow of death sounds pretty awful, doesn't it?'

Lexi wondered if Grandma thought that her 'valley of the shadow of death' was here and now.

'It says that I *walk through* the valley,' she went on. 'That means I'm only going to walk *through* it, Lexi. I don't have to stay there for ever.' Grandmother smiled happily. 'We pass through troubled times. We don't remain trapped in them. God is with us as we walk through them and come out on the other side.'

Grandma's face was beaming, 'Isn't that wonderful news, Lexi? I remind myself of that when things get too bad. We're only passing through. We're not meant to stay in trouble for ever.

'It's been difficult since your grandfather died. I've had to remind myself of this passage often.' Grandma shook her head. 'I have so much trouble remembering things these days, but I always seem to recall this verse whenever I need it.

'Getting old isn't easy.' Grandma's expression turned pensive. 'In fact, it seems to me, the hardest part of life is saved for last. Perhaps that's because we need so much knowledge and experience to cope with these final years of our lives.' Grandmother stroked Lexi's head again. 'Am I depressing you with this chatter of mine?'

Lexi shook her head. This was just like having Grandmother the way she used to be before her illness. 'Oh, no, Grandmother, I love talking to you.'

Grandmother's eyes misted. 'It's been wonderful staying here with you, your parents and Ben.' Her eyebrows knit together. 'Sometimes I feel like it's been a real hardship for you. But having a family that cares for me the way you do has been a real blessing.'

Lexi felt the tears catch at the back of her throat. Her mother had been right. Her grandmother *had* sensed their love.

Grandmother closed the Bible and patted the cover. 'I promised your mother I'd peel potatoes for supper, Lexi. Would you like to help me?'

'Could we make a raw potato sandwich?' Lexi asked excitedly. 'Like the ones Grandpa used to make?'

Grandma's eyes twinkled. 'Why, I do believe we could. Wouldn't a raw potato sandwich taste good right now!' She put her fingers to her lips. 'But don't tell your mother. She'll think we're ruining our appetite for supper.'

Together they made their way into the kitchen. Lexi's heart and mind felt lighter and brighter than they had in many weeks. This conversation with her grandmother was a gift from God; a bright spot to remember when Grandmother's memory faded again.

~ 3 ~

'The farmer's in his den, the farmer's in his den,
hi-ho . . .'

Lexi opened one eye when she felt a pair of small
cold hands on her cheeks. Ben stopped singing long
enough to announce, 'Time to get up, Lexi.' He
began humming again and turned his attention to
the knick-knacks on Lexi's dresser, 'Pretty,' he said
to himself.

'You're very cheerful this morning,' Lexi said with
a yawn. She swung her legs over the side of the bed
and stretched.

'Ben's happy,' he affirmed. He kept on humming
and fingering the figurines.

Lexi pulled on her dressing gown, lifted a brush
from her dresser and began to tug it through her hair.
'What makes you so happy this morning?'

'I don't know,' Ben shrugged his shoulders. 'Ben's just happy.' Then, much to Lexi's surprise, he added, 'I like having Grandma living with us.'

'You do, Ben?' Lexi sat down on the edge of her bed and stared at her little brother. She was amazed at Ben's announcement. Grandmother was special and wonderful when her mind was clear. Still, she was so unpredictable that Lexi assumed Ben would be confused by her behaviour. 'Don't you get mixed up by Grandma sometimes?'

Ben turned to face her. His brown eyes were wide. He nodded. 'Grandma does funny things.'

Lexi nodded too. 'Yes, she does.'

'Grandma says funny things.'

'She does that too,' Lexi agreed. 'Doesn't that bother you?'

Ben thought about it for a long moment, screwing his round little face into a mask of thoughtful consideration. 'No. I just like Grandma.'

Lexi sighed, wishing that she could have some of that marvellous acceptance that her little brother was displaying. Ben liked Grandmother in the house no matter what she did. How lucky for him – and for Grandma!

'I'm supposed to go and eat breakfast,' Ben announced, as he walked toward the door.

'Did Mum send you up to wake me up?' Lexi asked.

Ben nodded cheerfully and disappeared through the door.

Lexi stared after him. 'Little rascal,' she muttered

with a smile. She fell back on her bed. Ben always managed to make her think about things in new ways.

Every time she was bold enough to assume she knew more than her handicapped little brother, he proved her wrong. For one thing, Ben had a better view of Grandma's illness than Lexi did. He liked his grandmother. He didn't care how she behaved. He was glad she lived with them. It was as simple as that. Ben wasn't embarrassed, frightened or saddened by Grandmother's illness. He just accepted it.

Lexi closed her eyes tightly. 'Oh, God,' she whispered, 'Help me to be as accepting as Ben is. I know you're up there, Lord, and I know you're listening to me because you promised you would. But you seem so far away sometimes. When I get frightened, I don't know what to do, God. Are you there?'

Lexi closed her eyes tightly and tears squeezed from beneath her lashes. God never moved away from her. Lexi knew that. But sometimes she moved away from God.

Every time she allowed resentment, anger or frustration to overwhelm her it seemed she took a step backward, away from his presence.

Lexi pulled on her clothes in frustrated jerks. It was so awful to feel helpless! She wanted to help her grandmother and her family, but there was nothing she could do. Lexi wasn't sure that there was anyone else in the world who could understand the sort of frustration she felt.

Lexi walked downstairs, listening for activity in the

kitchen. Ben was talking to his mother in the living room. Grandmother was sitting alone at the kitchen table. As Lexi neared, she realised that there were tears on her grandmother's cheeks too!

'Grandma? What's wrong?'

Grandma Carson looked up from the bowl of cereal in front of her. Her eyes were moist and her nose was red. She looked very sad. 'Oh, Lexi,' she moaned. 'I just can't do it and I don't know why.'

Lexi was taken aback by the frustration in her grandmother's voice. She glanced at the cereal bowl. 'Are you having trouble eating, Grandma?'

Grandma Carson tugged at her white hair. 'I wanted to eat it,' she said, looking at the bowl forlornly. Lexi followed her grandmother's gaze to the soggy flakes. They seemed to be covered with a brown liquid. 'I always put something on my cereal,' Grandmother said, 'but, I couldn't remember what it was.' She stared at her coffee cup. 'So I used that. But it's not right. That's not what you put on cereal.'

'Oh, Grandma,' Lexi blurted. Grandmother had forgotten that it was milk she should put on her cereal! Even worse, she was clear enough to realise that she'd made a mistake, but didn't know how to correct it. Lexi took away the cereal bowl and emptied it into the bin. She rinsed out the bowl and poured in another helping of flakes with some fresh milk. 'There you go, Grandma, It's okay.'

'I should have known. I should have known.' Grandma Carson groaned, putting her hands to her temples. 'Why can't I remember these things, Lexi?'

Tears rolled down her cheeks and her hands trembled. Lexi slid her arm around her grandmother's shoulders and they both wept.

'Lexi, are you going to be at home this afternoon?' Mrs Leighton asked on Saturday.

'As far as I know,' Lexi said. 'I cleaned the cages at the kennel this morning.'

'Good. Would you mind staying here with Grandma for just a couple of hours? I've got a list of items to pick up. Ben needs new tennis shoes for one thing. I discovered this morning that his are far too small. That child is growing faster than the weeds in the garden.'

'Of course, Mum. I'll stay here with Grandma.'

It wasn't her first choice of Saturday afternoon activities, but Lexi knew how much her mother needed to get out of the house. Besides, Grandmother always took a long nap in the afternoon. It would be an opportunity for her to get her history report done.

'Great! I'll take Ben with me and we'll leave right away. I just checked on Grandma and she's all tucked into her bed for her nap. She didn't sleep very well last night so I expect that she'll sleep for an hour or two at least.'

After they had gone, Lexi got out her history book and her research notes. She spread them on the dining room table. From that vantage point, she could keep one eye on the staircase so that Grandmother couldn't sneak past her. Within minutes, Lexi was deeply engrossed in her project.

A tapping on the back door distracted her. When

she opened it, a young man carrying a suitcase full of magazines greeted her. It took her some moments to convince him that she could not buy anything from him. It was up to her mother.

It was nearly five o'clock when she finished her report. The telephone rang. It was Lexi's father. 'Is your mother there?'

'She took Ben shopping for tennis shoes.'

'And you're watching Grandma?'

'Yes. She's been sleeping all afternoon.' Lexi glanced at her wrist-watch. 'It's been almost three hours.'

'That doesn't sound like Grandma,' Mr Leighton commented. 'Have you checked on her?'

Lexi's eyes grew wide, 'No. I suppose I should have.'

'I'm sure everything's all right, Lexi. But why don't you just run upstairs to make sure she hasn't fallen or something.'

'Hang on Dad, I'll be right back.'

Lexi laid the telephone receiver on the table and took the stairs two at a time to her grandmother's room. She opened the door quietly so as not to disturb her if she was still asleep. Then Lexi's mouth dropped open. Grandmother's bed was empty!

She quickly looked around the room, but Grandmother was nowhere to be found. Running from room to room, she checked them all, but Grandmother was not there. Lexi ran back to the telephone. 'Dad, she's gone!'

'Have you looked everywhere?'

'Just upstairs. Let me look down here.'

'Where could she have gone?' Mr Leighton wondered, the alarm in his voice frightening Lexi even more.

'I don't know. I've been sitting at the dining room table all afternoon working on my history report. She couldn't have come down the stairs, without my seeing her. Except –' Lexi paused.

'Except what, Lexi?'

'There was a salesman at the back door. It only took a few minutes to get rid of him, but –'

'I'll be right home. Look around the garden.' Mr Leighton's voice was anxious.

'Oh Dad, I'm sorry.'

'It's not your fault, Lexi. I'll be home right away.'

Lexi hung up the phone and ran outside. 'Grandma! Grandma!' she called. She checked the attic then the basement, but her grandmother was nowhere to be found. Then Lexi went outside again not knowing where to look. There were very few places to hide in the Leighton garden. It was just an open expanse of lawn. She checked the tool shed and the garage, and was relieved to see her father pull up in the drive.

'She's not in the house, Dad, and she's not out here in the garden.'

'How long ago was the salesman here, Lexi?'

Lexi glanced at her watch. 'It was over an hour ago, Dad.'

Mr Leighton's mouth was set in a grim line. 'She could have gone a long way in an hour. I'm going to have to call the police.'

Lexi wanted to sink into the ground and die. *The*

police. It was all her fault. She should have been more careful.

Mr Leighton returned from the inside of the house within minutes. 'They're sending someone out, Lexi. After we hear what their plan is, we can head out in separate directions and look too. She could be anywhere.'

'Oh, Dad, what if she gets hurt?'

'Let's not think about that now, Lexi. We'll just concentrate on finding her.'

'She was wearing her nightdress, Dad,' Lexi blurted.

'Maybe that will work to our advantage, Lexi. At least she'll be noticed. Someone is more apt to pick her up if she looks as if she's disoriented and confused. Why don't you head south and if you haven't found her in thirty minutes, come back to the house.' Mr Leighton indicated that Lexi would feel better about the whole thing if she could be of some help right away.

Lexi nodded and ran for her bike. She kicked up the stand and swung on to the seat. As she rode, her mind spun. There were a hundred places Grandma could have gone in a town this size. Lexi darted through the alleys and zig-zagged down the streets with her eyes peeled for a sight of her grandmother. Nothing.

Lexi was almost to the schoolhouse when she considered turning back. Then she felt the urge to ride just one more block.

Though it was Saturday, the school car-park was full. The school was hosting a regional art show, and cars were pulling in and out in every direction. To

Lexi's horror, in the middle of the congestion stood her grandmother. She was shuffling from one side of the car-park to the other. Lexi pressed forward on her bike, spinning pebbles and gravel from her wheels.

'Grandma, Grandma!' she called at the top of her lungs. It was her grandmother who had caused the congestion in the car-park. Everyone was trying to drive around her. Some had stopped, making an effort to talk to her.

Lexi pulled up on her bike and jumped off.

'Madam, this is a dangerous place to be wandering around,' a gentlemen was saying. 'Are you looking for the craft show? It's inside. Perhaps I could help you . . .'

Grandma stared at the man blankly, not comprehending. Lexi moved toward her and grasped her elbow firmly, 'Grandmother, it's Lexi.'

Mrs Carson's eyes flickered with faint recognition. 'You got lost, Grandmother. It's time for us to go home now.'

Lexi felt her heart thudding like a sledgehammer in her chest.

'Hey, do you know this lady?' another man asked.

'Yes. She has Alzheimer's disease and she gets very confused. She wandered away from the house.'

'Oh.' Understanding dawned on the faces of the adults clustered around them.

'Is there anyone we should phone? Is there anything we can do?' someone asked.

'Would you please ring my father?' Lexi gave them the number. 'Tell him that I've found Grandmother, and ask him to pick her up at the school. Thank you very much.'

It took all of Lexi's strength to hold back the tears. She refused to cry. Not here. She would not be embarrassed by her grandmother. As she clung to her arm, Lexi remembered that her mother had told her Alzheimer's was not anything to be embarrassed by.

Lexi had admitted that Grandmother had Alzheimer's to this group of strangers and no one had laughed. They had nodded their heads in understanding.

What had seemed odd and abnormal behaviour suddenly became understandable in the light of Grandmother's disease. It hadn't been embarrassing to admit that her grandmother had Alzheimer's. In fact, it had made Lexi feel free. It felt good to explain Grandmother's behaviour and not be ashamed. It felt good to have people understand the problem.

Lexi slipped her arm around Grandmother's shoulders. 'Don't be scared. Dad's coming soon.'

Grace Carson nodded her head forlornly, 'I wanted to go for a walk,' she explained, 'But I don't like it. It's too crowded here.'

A soft smile crossed Lexi's face. 'It *is* crowded here, Grandma. Next time you want to go for a walk, ask me to take you.'

'That's a good idea,' Grandma said agreeably.

Just then Jim Leighton arrived in his car. He helped Grandma into the back seat and Lexi followed. Then her dad tossed her bike into the boot.

'Are you all right?'

'I'm fine, Dad. Just fine.'

'I'm sorry, love. I know how hard this is on you,' her father began.

Lexi held up a hand. 'Don't be, Dad. This wasn't as bad as I thought it would be; I think I'm learning.'

They rode back to the house in silence.

~ 4 ~

'I'm starving!' Binky announced.

'Me, too,' Egg echoed. 'A burger and chips would taste marvellous right now.'

'And a milk shake and onion rings,' Jennifer added.

Harry and Todd nodded in agreement. Lexi, who was standing nearby, was silent. She was hungry too. It had been a long time since she had been to the Hamburger Shack with the gang. Ever since she and Todd had split up, Lexi had avoided groups that included him. It was just too painful.

'You're joining us, aren't you Lexi?' Binky pleaded, her eyes warm and hopeful. 'You haven't been out with us for such a long time.'

Lexi was tempted to say no. But considering what waited for her at home, she decided she needed a break. Surely going to the Hamburger Shack with

Todd couldn't be any more painful than being at home with Grandma! The memories of the wonderful times they'd shared together at the Shack couldn't hurt that much.

'Oh, I suppose,' Lexi relented.

Binky and Jennifer grinned at each other. Lexi's gaze darted toward Todd. He really did look great, Lexi thought to herself. His golden blond hair had grown a little longer and curled at the nape of his neck. He wore a white shirt and black jeans that showed off his athletic build. He even had an early tan. Lexi's heart quivered.

'I don't know about the rest of you, but I'm starved,' Jennifer announced. She spun around on her heel and slipped her arm through Todd's. They strolled off together, laughing and joking. Jennifer waved back over her shoulder. 'Come on you guys. Hurry up.'

Jennifer said something which amused Todd. He threw back his head and laughed.

Watching them, Lexi felt a pang of jealousy. Even though she knew that Jennifer and Todd were just friends, it hurt her to see them together. She should be the one walking with Todd, smiling up at him in that way!

'Are you coming, Lexi?' Binky asked as the rest of the group moved off.

Lexi waved her arm, 'I can't, Binky, I just can't.' Abruptly she spun around and ran in the other direction.

Lexi walked for nearly thirty minutes before she went home. When she reached the house, her father was there waiting for her.

'What are you doing home so early, Dad?'

'I have a meeting to attend,' he explained. 'Come here, Lexi,' he patted the seat next to him. 'Sit down and talk to me.'

Lexi sank into the spot and leaned her head against her father's shoulder, closed her eyes and sighed.

'I've been worrying about you, Lexi,' Mr Leighton commented.

'About me?' Lexi was surprised. Her parents had so much to worry about that she hadn't considered the fact that they might be worrying about her.

'You've been very withdrawn lately. Sometimes I look at you and I see an expression on your face that tells me you're miserable.'

'Oh, I'm okay,' Lexi began.

Mr Leighton shook his head. 'Don't try to tell me otherwise, Lexi. I know what it's been like around here. In fact, the meeting that your mother and I are going to this afternoon concerns a new support group that's starting at the hospital for families attempting to care for Alzheimer's patients in their homes. Your mother and I are eager to participate because, frankly, we've decided we need all the help we can get.'

It seemed odd for her father who already was a doctor – a veterinarian – to be admitting that he didn't know all there was to know about medicine.

Her father looked at her intently. 'We'd like you to come along.'

'Me?' Lexi shook her head. 'No way. I get enough about Alzheimer's here at home. I don't want to hear other people talking about it too.'

45

'That's not the point,' her father said patiently. 'Support groups provide an opportunity to talk to other people who are in the same situation as you are, to give each other support and advice. It can be comforting to know that you're not all alone with your problems, Lexi.'

Lexi *did* feel alone. Completely alone.

Lexi thought back to the sight of Todd and Jennifer walking together down the street. How could they ever begin to understand how her life had come apart?

'Lexi, I think it's important that you come.' Her father's voice was firm.

She shrugged her shoulders and nodded her head. 'All right.' Why not do one more thing she didn't want to do? Her life was a nightmare anyway.

What did it matter?

The hospital corridors smelled of antiseptic. Lexi's stomach turned nervously as she followed her parents to a small meeting room lined with chairs. There were several adults in the room, all of them looking equally nervous. Lexi glanced around. There were no teenagers. She cast a panicky look at her father.

A white-uniformed nurse caught Lexi's worried look. 'Don't worry. There are other teenagers here. Your room is next door. The group leader's name is Mary Anne.'

Relief flooded Lexi. She hurried into the next room. There were several teenagers, and Lexi's gaze fell on a tall, thin boy who reminded her a little of Egg.

Two girls sat on the couch. One girl was laughing and giggling with the tall thin boy. The other girl sat quietly with her head down and her hands folded in her lap, withdrawn from everyone around her. Lexi recognised something of herself in the girl's manner.

A young nurse stood up. 'Welcome. My name is Mary Anne. I'd like to tell you a few things about myself. First of all, I understand the kinds of situations in which your families are finding themselves. I grew up with a grandfather who suffered from Alzheimer's disease. Though he didn't live in our home, he lived in a flat nearby. My family took sole responsibility for his care.

'As a teenager, I spent many afternoons and evenings with my grandfather, making sure that he didn't turn on the stove, cut himself or burn himself with a match.' Mary Anne's eyes grew warm and sympathetic, 'I loved my grandfather very much. That love did not stop when he was diagnosed as having Alzheimer's. It's very frustrating, however, to love someone who is losing his or her ability to return love. We're here today to help you cope with the kinds of things you might be facing in your family.

'Now, so we can get to know and understand each other a little better, I'd like each of you to introduce yourself and to tell us about your family member suffering from Alzheimer's disease.'

She smiled at the tall, thin boy. 'Why don't we start with you?'

The boy's face blushed beetroot and Lexi was reminded again of her friend Egg. 'M-My name is

R–Robert,' he stuttered. 'My grandpa has Alzheimer's disease too. M-My father is an only child and when Grandpa got sick, he decided that we should take care of him at our house. He just moved in last week, but we're already pretty fed up.' The boy dropped his chin to his chest. 'That's all.'

The bubbly girl on the couch spoke next. 'My name is Amy. My grandmother has had Alzheimer's disease for four years. She's really been pretty good until just lately. Now she's beginning to forget lots of things. She doesn't live with us yet, but that's what my parents are talking about. I have a baby brother at home and they're worried about him. They aren't sure how Grandma might react to a baby in the house.'

Amy's face fell. 'I don't really like the idea of having her there.' A blush seeped on to her cheeks, 'I know this is weird and probably wrong, but I have this feeling I might catch this disease from her or something. I don't ever want to act like that.'

Mary Anne interrupted, 'Just so that you'll feel better, Amy, there is no way that you can "catch" Alzheimer's disease. It's inherited in about ten to thirty percent of the cases, otherwise, it's a random disease.'

'Are you sure?' Amy asked, still looking doubtful.

'I'm positive.'

Lexi could tell that Amy was relieved.

The silent girl next to Amy did not lift her head. Lexi waited for a moment. When the girl didn't speak, she went ahead with her own story.

'My name is Lexi Leighton, and my grandmother has lived with us ever since my grandfather died.

She's very forgetful and confused. Grandma's mixed up about eighty percent of the time now. I have a little brother at home who's got Down's syndrome and he seems to be accepting this better than I am.'

Lexi's voice wavered. 'I even broke up with my boy-friend over my grandmother's illness. He couldn't understand how tough it is to have someone like that living in your house. He didn't see that sometimes, even when you don't want to be impatient, you sound as though you are.'

Lexi felt tears tickle the back of her eyelids. 'I'm a Christian. I've been asking God to help me get through this.' She sighed. 'Sometimes I think you get to a point where God is the only one who *can* help you. That's where we're at right now.'

Mary Anne nodded and gave Lexi an affirming smile. Lexi sighed and sank into her chair. It had actually felt good to say those things, to admit to someone who could understand how rough her life had been. Now everyone's eyes fell on the quiet girl on the couch. She sat with her hands woven together in her lap.

'My name is Nan.' She murmured so softly that Lexi had to strain to hear her. 'And my father has recently been diagnosed as having Alzheimer's disease.'

Her father! Lexi's heart went out to the girl. How awful. 'My dad is thirty-six years old,' Nan continued. 'He's a salesman. He travels on the road a lot, but he won't be able to continue because my mother's worried that he won't be safe driving. He's not bad yet, but nobody in our family knows what to expect.'

Tears welled up in Nan's eyes. 'My Mum is looking for work to support our family, but she cries at night because she doesn't want to put Dad in a nursing home. She wants to stay at home and take care of him herself.' Nan sighed wearily. 'I told my mum I'd help her take care of Dad, but I'm scared. I don't want my daddy to change!'

Lexi felt flooded with selfishness. How could she feel sorry for herself when this poor girl had a problem so much more serious?

Mary Anne spoke. 'I want each of you to tell me something about your feelings concerning your family member's illness. Tell us something that you've never told anyone else before – an emotion, a thought. Maybe it's something you're a little bit ashamed to admit. We'll all understand. We each have someone in our family with the same problem. Robert, why don't we start with you?'

Robert's face turned red. It took him a long time to speak. When he did, his voice was low and shaky. 'My grandfather asked me the same question about fifty times yesterday. Finally, I got tired of answering and I yelled at him. Now I feel guilty. I shouldn't have done that. He couldn't help it.'

'It's not unusual to become impatient, Robert, with someone who asks questions over and over again. The Alzheimer's victim may have no recent memory. Each time they ask a question and get the answer, they're viewing it as original information. Your grandfather thinks he's asking that question for the very first time. Don't feel guilty. We're all human, you know.'

Robert nodded.

'Amy, do you have any thoughts you'd like to share?'

Amy looked serious. 'Well, there's something that does bother me. My parents spend so much time with my grandparents that they don't ever have time for me any more. I suppose I miss my parents.'

Lexi found herself nodding. She'd had the same thoughts.

'Nan, do you have anything you'd like to say?' Mary Anne spoke gently.

Everyone knew that Nan's wounds were the freshest and the deepest right now. No one wanted to upset her. Suddenly, Nan burst out, 'Sometimes when I think about what's happening, I'm so angry, I wish my dad were dead,' Nan blurted. She looked horrified at what she'd said. 'I'm sorry. I should never have said that.'

Mary Anne moved nearer the girl and put her hand on her shoulder. 'You're simply angry. You have every right to feel that way. Your life is changing and you don't want it to. You don't have to be angry with your father. He didn't choose this or cause this. On the other hand don't try to hide your anger or suppress it. It's perfectly normal.'

'Normal?' Nan looked up at Mary Anne with a flicker of hope in her eyes. 'I'm not a horrible person to feel that way?'

'You're a very normal person in a very bad circumstance,' Mary Anne said softly. 'Lexi? Do you have something you'd like to say?'

Lexi chewed on her lower lip. 'I think what bothers

me most is that I'm embarrassed all the time,' she admitted. 'I don't like having my friends come over to see my grandmother the way she is now. I want to remember her as she was when she was healthy. I don't want my friends to think of her as a silly mixed-up old woman.' Lexi's chin came out indignantly. 'She's too nice a lady for that.'

'So in one way you're embarrassed yet in another you're trying to protect your grandmother's image?' Mary Anne paraphrased.

'I suppose you could say that,' Lexi admitted. 'I hadn't thought about it quite that way before.'

'Well, I have to tell you that you're all perfectly normal,' Mary Anne smiled. 'You haven't said one unusual thing or expressed one feeling that I didn't expect to hear. You're all just fine. If we don't do another thing in this group other than to make you realise that, the group will have been a success. I'm sure that all of you are holding lots of thoughts and feelings inside. It will feel good to talk about them, to get them out in the open. Does anyone have anything else they'd like to say about the feelings that they've had lately?'

Lexi looked from Mary Anne's kind face to Nan's tear-stained one. Hesitantly, she raised her hand.

'I don't know if hearing how I've been feeling lately will help you or not,' she began, glancing at Nan, 'but I've been pretty scared. I've really had a good life. My parents love me and we've always had a nice home and I've got good exam grades. Even though my brother has Down's syndrome, Ben's such a cute little kid that he's taught us a lot of good things about people who have handicaps.

'Ever since Grandmother came to live with us, I feel as if I've lost something. It started when my grandfather died. I thought that was the worst thing in the world that could ever happen. Then, when I found out that grandmother was ill, I was *sure* that was the worst thing that ever could happen to me.' She paused for a moment before continuing.

'I began to question my own faith. My boy-friend told me he thought I was a hypocrite. He accused me of saying I was a Christian but not really acting like one.'

Lexi smiled weakly, 'The outcome of that was that I lost a boy-friend, but my faith is growing stronger than ever. He did me a favour by making me take a hard look at myself. What I'm really trying to say is that though I've lost a lot, I feel I can understand what everybody else is going through a little better.'

The group was silent, considering what Lexi had said. Suddenly, they were all talking, sharing the feelings they'd kept inside.

A buzzer went off minutes later and Mary Anne held up her hand. 'Our time is already up,' she said. 'I'd like to thank each of you for sharing with us as you have today. And I'd like to invite each of you to come back next week. I think we have a lot of ground to cover. We can do it together.'

Robert stood up and walked out of the room. Nan moved towards Mary Anne who began to speak to her quietly.

Bubbly Amy turned to Lexi. 'Can I talk to you for a minute?'

'Of course,' Lexi said. She liked the girl's sparkling eyes and bright smile.

'I just wanted to tell you that I'm a Christian too. I was wondering if we could pray for each other. I think that would help. Don't you?' Amy looked at Lexi hopefully.

Lexi felt a smile building deep within her. It spilled across her face, 'I'd like that very much, Amy.'

'Good. I think what we need right now are others praying for us. I'll pray for you this week, Lexi. I promise.' Just then, Amy's parents called to her from the corridor. 'I have to go. See you next week!' Amy smiled and waved.

Lexi went to find her parents, feeling both pleased and happy. Maybe this group wasn't such a bad idea after all. She'd said some things that she'd been afraid to say before. No one had scolded her. They'd all seemed to understand. What's more, she'd found a friend who would pray for her. Lexi was smiling when she met her parents.

'Don't you look happy!' Mrs Leighton said. 'It's so good to see you smile.'

Lexi nodded. It felt good to *be* smiling. For the first time in ages, she felt there might be some hope for their family after all.

~ 5 ~

Lexi took her time putting away her music after the Emerald Tones' rehearsal. She worked slowly until she was sure that Todd and Harry had left the practice room.

All the things she had once loved, such as rehearsing with the Emerald Tones and taking photos for the *River Review* had become difficult chores now that she and Todd were avoiding one another.

Her footsteps were slow as she made her way outside. Lexi rounded the corner of the school and nearly tripped over Egg McNaughton as he balanced, head first, in a dustbin.

Lexi could tell it was Egg by the long legs and the weird combination of blue socks and orange shoe laces. Every few seconds, an aluminium can would come flying out of the dustbin.

'Egg? What are you doing?'

His head popped out of the bin like a grubby jack-in-the-box. 'Hi, Lexi. I'm looking for cans. Want to help?'

Lexi wrinkled her nose. 'No thanks. I'm not into . . . rubbish.'

'You should be.' Egg began to gather the cans on the ground into a large paper sack. His face was flushed and indignant. 'You'd never believe the things you find in a dustbin!'

Lexi eyed him warily. 'What's got into you, Egg?'

'Look at all the waste!' He pointed to a small pile on the pavement. 'There are pencils and erasers – only half used, aluminium cans, paper, cardboard. All these things can be recycled. That's what I'm doing. I needed some extra money, so I decided to take aluminium cans to the recycling centre. I can't believe how much reusable stuff the students at Cedar River throw away!'

'You're probably right, Egg, but what can one person do about it?'

Egg's face was contorted with determination. 'I don't know – yet. But I'll think of something. Right now I have to go through all the rubbish bins outside the school. Don't you want to help me?'

Digging in someone else's rubbish was the last thing Lexi felt like doing, but being alone to think about the turns her life had taken sounded even worse.

'Sure. Why not? You dig, I'll hold the sack for you.'

Egg gave Lexi a pleased grin and loped to the next dustbin.

'You know,' Egg began as he dug through the day's rubbish, 'I've been reading a lot about this recycling business. I'm going to look into it more over the summer.'

'Have you got any other plans for the summer?' Lexi asked. It was hard to believe the school year was almost over.

'None yet.' Egg's voice was muffled as he bent into another bin.

'Not even with Anna Marie?' Lexi asked impishly, referring to Egg's attraction to their mutual friend.

Egg popped out of the dustbin. His expression showed real concern. 'I worry about Anna Marie sometimes. She's got really thin.'

Anna Marie had been diagnosed as anorexic. Her eating habits were bad and she'd lost a lot of weight. No matter what anyone said, it was almost impossible to get Anna Marie to eat anything – even when she went to the Hamburger Shack. 'I worry about her too,' Lexi admitted. 'I thought after she'd seen a doctor, things would improve.' She sighed. 'Why does everything have to be so difficult?'

Egg was pensive a minute. He surprised her by saying, 'Do you know who I really miss? Peggy Madison. When is she coming home?'

Lexi drew a sharp breath. Peggy was one of her closest friends. It had nearly broken Lexi's heart when Peggy had become pregnant and gone to live with her uncle until the baby was born. Very few people in Cedar River other than Todd, Lexi, and Peggy's boy-friend Chad had known the true reason for Peggy's departure.

'Soon, I think. Some time before the summer is over.' Peggy's baby was due soon and Lexi knew that Peggy was anxious to return to her home and friends. That would be something to look forward to this summer.

'Minda Hannaford and Jerry Randall are still going together, I see,' Egg muttered. He seemed determined to talk about all their mutual friends. It was obviously difficult for him to talk about Minda. Egg had had a crush on her for a long time. Minda, on the other hand, barely acknowledged that Egg existed.

After he'd searched all the school dustbins, Lexi helped Egg carry his bags of aluminium cans home. Binky was sitting on the back steps studying when they arrived.

'What are you two doing?' Binky wondered, staring suspiciously at her brother. 'Has Egg got you doing something weird, Lexi?'

Lexi shrugged and held up a can. 'We're recycling.'

Binky threw her book on to a step, as if the subject was of no interest to her. 'I wouldn't mind a milk shake right now. Anybody care to join me?'

Egg was suddenly alert. 'Food? You say something about food?'

Binky and Lexi laughed out loud. As they walked together towards the Hamburger Shack, Lexi watched her friends admiringly. Egg's long-legged, ambling gait was awkward but swift. Binky's short legs churned to keep up with him.

Lexi was filled with a surge of gratitude. Not

everything in her life had turned sour. She still had the greatest friends in the world.

The next afternoon, Lexi stopped at Mrs Waverly's office after school. She was busy at her desk. Half a dozen pens and pencils sprouted from the pale blonde curls piled on top of her head. Lexi knocked on the door that stood ajar. When Mrs Waverly looked up, two pencils slipped from her hair and clattered to the floor.

'Oh, Lexi, come in,' Mrs Waverly's eyes lit up with pleasure. She cleared off a stool next to her desk and patted the seat. 'Sit down. It's been such a long time since you've stopped to see me. What can I do for you?'

'Nothing – r-really,' Lexi stammered. 'I just had a few minutes and I saw you in here alone.'

'Well, I'm happy to see you.' Mrs Waverly looked at Lexi fondly. 'You've been quiet in music classes lately. I haven't had an opportunity to chat to you.' A frown passed over Mrs Waverly's features. 'In fact, I've been a little worried about you, Lexi.'

'Worried? About me?' Lexi asked, somewhat startled. How could Mrs Waverly know what had been going on her life? Lexi had been making every effort to keep it a secret.

'Yes, dear. You've seemed rather depressed.' When Lexi didn't respond, Mrs Waverly continued, 'You're usually such a bubbly, happy girl, always participating in class. Lately, I've had to look twice to see if you were even in class. That's not like you, Lexi. Is there something wrong?'

'No. N–Nothing is wrong,' Lexi stammered, feeling guilty for the lie. 'I've just been quiet.'

Mrs Waverly gazed at her intently. 'I know better than that, Lexi. You're not a very good liar. You might as well tell me the truth.'

Lexi looked ashamed. 'It's that obvious?'

The teacher nodded. 'You're normally very outgoing – a pleasure to have in class. When you almost disappear into the woodwork, I'm bound to sense that something's wrong.'

Lexi hooked her heels around the legs of the stool, and slumped forward dejectedly. 'I have been a little depressed lately. My grandfather died.'

'I'd heard that. I'm very sorry, Lexi.'

'At the time, I thought it was the worst thing in the world that could ever happen to our family, but it's not. Sometimes I think Grandpa was the lucky one.'

'That's a strong statement, Lexi. What do you mean?'

Lexi ran her fingers through her hair. She could feel tears welling up, but she didn't want to cry in front of her teacher. 'My grandfather was healthy for many years. Then he died suddenly,' she explained. 'Now, Grandmother, on the other hand –'

'I understand your grandmother is living with you,' Mrs Waverly interjected.

'Yes. But she's dying, too, Mrs Waverly. Not the same way my grandfather did. It's her mind that's dying. She has Alzheimer's disease,' Lexi continued. 'That's why I think Grandpa was the lucky one. He *lived* until he died. Grandma's dying a little every day and living through it. Each day she's a bit more disorientated, confused and forgetful. Each day she loses some small part of herself that she'll never recover.

'Her personality is changing. My grandmother used to be the sweetest, kindest woman in the world. Now we find her talking to herself or arguing with her reflection in the mirror. She's very stubborn. My mother can't always get her to do what she should.' Lexi sighed heavily. 'I feel sorry for my mum and dad, too. They take turns staying up at night listening for Grandma so she doesn't wander out of her room and get disorientated. Last week, Dad came home from work with a strong-box. We have to keep the knobs from the stove, sharp kitchen knives, scissors and matches under lock and key so my grandmother doesn't get them and hurt herself.

'Sometimes I have dreams at night that my room is full of smoke, that Grandma has left the stove on and started a fire.'

The words poured out of Lexi in a flood. 'My little brother Ben doesn't seem to be as affected by all of this much as the rest of us. He is confused by her behaviour sometimes, but he is able to accept it with less difficulty. He likes to have Grandma play with him, but sometimes the games he chooses are too hard for her.' Lexi's voice broke.

'Ben is barely nine years old and he has Down's syndrome. And the games he chooses are too complicated for my grandmother to play!'

'Oh, Lexi, I had no idea.'

'Nobody does,' Lexi said matter-of-factly. 'Anyone

who hasn't lived with Alzheimer's in their home can't have any idea what it's like. The person you love disappears before your eyes and you wear out trying to take care of her.' Lexi shuddered. 'For a long time I thought that our family was all alone in this.'

'And now you've changed your mind?' Mrs Waverly asked carefully.

Lexi nodded, 'A little bit. We're going to a support group at the hospital. I've met some others my age who have grandparents with Alzheimer's in their homes.' Lexi's eyes showed her anguish. 'I even met a girl whose *father* was just diagnosed as having Alzheimer's. It's just so hard, Mrs Waverly . . . so *hard*!'

The kind teacher bowed her head and folded her hands across the top of her desk. 'I'm so sorry I didn't speak to you sooner, Lexi. I saw something was troubling you, but I thought it would work itself out. I had no idea the depth of your problems at home.'

'I didn't mean any of it to show,' Lexi admitted.

Mrs Waverly smiled faintly. 'It was bound to show, Lexi. I've watched you interact with your friends lately. It's not the same.'

'You mean . . .'

Mrs Waverly nodded. 'I mean Todd. What's happened, Lexi? You both look as though you've lost your best friend.'

Lexi stared at her tennis shoes. Finally she muttered, 'I think maybe we did each lose our best friend.'

'Todd and you had a disagreement?'

Lexi nodded slowly. 'Over Grandmother.'

Mrs Waverly's dark eyebrows arched in surprise. 'Over your grandmother? How's that?'

'It's hard to explain,' Lexi began. 'It all started when Todd accused me of being a hypocrite.'

Mrs Waverly's expression was incredulous.

'At first it just hurt my feelings, but Todd was right. He accused me of telling others that they should accept and love people as they are. Then he pointed out that I wasn't doing that with my grandmother. It took me a while, but I began to realise that he was right. I had to take a long, hard look at what I believed about God and about being a Christian. That's the only thing that's got me – our entire family – through this thing with Grandmother. God's strength is the only strength we have any more.'

'Then I think Todd did you a favour, Lexi.'

'But it didn't end there,' she continued. 'Todd came over again before I'd had a chance to explain to him that he was right – that I'd finally accepted Grandmother's disease.'

Lexi's eyes clouded. 'Grandma's like a little child most of the time. That's how we've had to treat her. I took Grandmother to her room for a nap so we could talk when he came over the last time. He accused me of treating her like a child, and he was very upset. He said I was trying to keep her hidden. I don't think he'd ever seen anyone behave quite like my grandma did that day. I really think it scared and frustrated him.' Lexi smiled resignedly. 'I know it scared and frustrated *me* for a long time. Anyway, we had a terrible misunderstanding. Todd left, and I expect you know the rest.'

63

'And you've been awkward with one another ever since. No real communication between you, right?'

Lexi nodded. 'There's a big wall between us that neither of us can overcome. I don't know how to explain to Todd the changes that have happened in my life. I have a feeling that Todd is waiting for me to make the first move. So here we are – no longer friends.'

'I don't think that's quite true, Lexi,' Mrs Waverly said, 'I think you and Todd are very dear friends.'

Lexi gave a short laugh. 'Fine friends! We don't even speak any more. We hardly look at each other. And we've made the rest of our friends uncomfortable around us. It's almost as if we're forcing them to choose sides between us.'

'Have you asked that of them?'

'No, it just seems to happen that way.'

'That's because they like you both very much, Lexi, and they don't want to hurt your feelings. It seems to me the only way to heal the difficulties the rest of your friends are having is to heal your differences with Todd.'

A tear coursed down Lexi's cheek. 'I wish I could, Mrs Waverly. I wish I could go back to the time before my grandfather died when everything was perfect.'

Mrs Waverly put her hand on Lexi's arm and smiled. 'Memory is a wonderful thing, Lexi. It filters out all the bad times and allows us to remember the good ones. If I'd asked you if your life was perfect back then, you would have shaken your head. You'd have told me of all the hard work at school, all the housework your mother was giving you at home, what tricks your classmates were up to. You would not have said that your life was perfect.'

'Maybe not. But it was certainly better than what's happening to me now.'

'This too will pass,' Mrs Waverly assured her.

Lexi looked up, her eyes brimming with tears now. 'Grandma said something like that. She read to me the passage about "walking through the valley of the shadow of death and fearing no evil."'

'The Twenty-third Psalm.' Mrs Waverly nodded.

'Grandma pointed out that we were only walking *through* the valley, that we would come out on the other side. Do you think I'm ever going to come out on the other side of this one, Mrs Waverly?'

'I'm positive you will. The biggest mistake a person can make is to give up hope. Life is like an ever-changing mosaic. There are good times and bad. Sun and clouds. Feast and famine. Time passes. Things change. You'll see.'

The teacher's words were comforting.

Lexi told herself she was only walking *through* this time of trouble. Soon, with God's help, she'd come out of this valley.

'Lexi,' Mrs Waverly spoke again. 'I'm going to remember you and your family in my prayers – Todd too. He's a good friend. And I believe he was sincerely trying to help you, not hurt you.'

'I know that now, Mrs Waverly, I really do.' It was all a dreadful mistake. Lexi just had to work out how to take back the ugly words that she'd said.

* * *

'When are we going to have supper, Lexi?' Grandma asked. She was sitting at the kitchen table.

'We ate a half-an-hour ago, Grandma,' Lexi said patiently.

'Oh, we did. Oh, my, my.' Grandma sat quietly for a few moments as Lexi wiped down the work-top.

'When are we going to have supper, Lexi?' Grandma asked, 'I'm hungry.'

'We just ate, Grandma,' Lexi said again. 'I've just finished cleaning the kitchen.'

'Oh.'

Lexi counted to ten, trying to remain calm, when Grandma asked again, 'When are we going to have supper, Lexi?'

Lexi glanced at her mother for help. Mrs Leighton stood and put an arm around Grandma Carson. 'Why don't we get away from the kitchen. I believe it's reminding you of supper and you've already eaten.'

'I have? Oh,' Grandma seemed to process the information, then promptly forget it. 'I'm very hungry.'

Lexi finished cleaning up, then turned off the kitchen light. When she walked into the living room, her mother was there waiting. 'Just hang in there,' she said, giving Lexi a squeeze. 'It can drive you crazy, but –'

'It's all right, I'm getting used to it. Mary Anne told us at the support group that people with Alzheimer's will ask the same questions over and over again because they honestly don't realise they've just asked the same question. It's like brand new information to them. Grandma doesn't remember that she's already

66

had supper. If I thought I were hungry, I'd be asking too.'

Mrs Leighton gave her daughter a hug. 'You've come a long way, Lexi – from an angry, frightened girl into a patient, loving one.'

'I'm trying, Mum.'

'I know. And I'm proud of you. It's hard to express how proud I am.'

As Lexi went upstairs she was smiling. She was trying to be more patient and loving, and it seemed to be working.

She had help now. The group at the hospital had been good for her. People had offered to pray too. And God was with her. That's what a 'support network' was. It might not seem like much to an outsider or an unbeliever, Lexi mused, but she knew that with God on her side things were going to turn out all right.

Sunlight played on Lexi's eyelids. She gave a giant yawn and stretched like a cat before crawling out of bed. She hummed as she took her shower and dressed for school. She was still humming when she met her brother Ben on the upstairs landing.

'Lexi's happy?' Ben inquired, looking up at his sister. 'Lexi's singing.'

'I'm humming, Ben. Music without words.'

'Ben can hum,' he announced, making a buzzing sound like a large bee.

Lexi smiled at him. She felt wonderful this morning. She was so light-hearted she could hardly explain the radical change. Maybe those prayers of Amy and

Mrs Waverly were working. Whatever the reason, Lexi was grateful as she went into the kitchen.

Grandma Carson was alone there. She was still dressed in her nightdress and dressing gown, though she wore high heels. She was standing at the stove, but not cooking. She was talking to her reflection in the bottom of the saucepan. After so many days and weeks of feeling anger, the pitiful sight no longer upset Lexi. It only made her sad.

'Good morning, Grandma,' Lexi said. She gently took the saucepan from her grandmother and set it on the stove. 'How are you this morning?'

Impulsively, Lexi took her grandmother in her arms and held her in a warm hug. She was surprised at her grandmother's response – she clung to her as if she were a life raft in the middle of the ocean. Lexi pressed her cheek against her grandmother's and they stood a few moments swaying gently back and forth.

'I love you, Grandma,' Lexi whispered. 'I love you so much, and you're very, very precious. Just because you get mixed up sometimes doesn't mean we don't love you.'

Grandmother's arms tightened around her. It wasn't until Ben burst into the kitchen making his bee-like sound that Grandmother's grip lessened and Lexi released her.

Lexi realised that there was only one message that would get through to Grandmother these days – the message of love. Grandma smiled brightly and touched Lexi's cheeks. Though she didn't speak, Lexi knew that the hug had reached through her grandmother's confusion and touched her heart.

Lexi was silent as she ate breakfast. The food was tasteless, seasoned as it was with Lexi's regret. There were so many days that Lexi could have offered her grandmother love and hadn't. But it was not too late. Lexi had seen how her grandmother responded to her affectionate hug. It was definitely not too late for Lexi to show Grandmother how much she loved her.

~ 6 ~

The doorbell rang.

I wonder who that is? Lexi thought. They weren't expecting guests that she knew of. She peeked out of the front window. Jennifer Golden and Binky McNaughton stood on the porch. Lexi's heart gave a leap as she threw open the door. 'Jennifer. Binky. Hi! What's up?'

Jennifer and Binky exchanged sheepish glances. 'We hadn't been over here for so long, we decided to come for a visit,' Binky said, looking suddenly shy. 'I hope you don't mind.'

Lexi smiled broadly. 'Mind? Of course not! Come on in.'

Lexi sensed that the two girls expected to be turned away at the door. It wasn't an unreasonable expectation, Lexi mused, considering the way she'd behaved toward her friends recently.

But she was done with that now. She was delighted her friends had come.

'I'm so glad you came. I've been bored.'

Lexi led the girls into the living room where Grandmother Carson sat in her rocking chair. The memory flashed across Lexi's mind of the circumstance under which the girls had met her grandmother before – arguing with herself in the mirror.

Thankfully, today Grandma's mind was clear. She sat crocheting a scarf of blue angora wool. Her hands, usually still, were flying over the work.

'Grandma, I'd like you to meet my friends. Do you remember Jennifer and Binky?'

Grandma Carson looked up from her scarf and her eyes brightened. 'How nice to have company.'

'We go to school together, Grandma,' Lexi explained.

Grandma laid down her crocheting. 'I remember my school-days,' she said dreamily. 'I lived on a farm and went to a country school. Do you girls know anything about country schools?'

Binky and Jennifer both shook their heads. Lexi sensed they were waiting to see what would happen next.

'The farm was only two miles from the school, so I walked every day. I packed my lunch in a little tin bucket with a handle. Some days I'd bring sandwiches made with fresh bread and homemade jam,' Grandma reminisced.

'I always loved the days when my mother baked. Her doughnuts were the very best. I loved her cakes too, but the icing got pretty messy by lunchtime at school.

'The teacher would always be at the school before we arrived, stoking the stove and carrying water.' Grandma chuckled. 'Quite a bit different from school today, don't you think?'

Binky and Jennifer nodded. Lexi knew they wondered about the change in Grandma since their earlier visit.

'My teacher was very fussy about penmanship,' Grandmother said. 'She'd have the little ones practise their writing while she was giving the bigger children their lessons. I'm still a pretty good writer today, aren't I Lexi?'

'You certainly are, Grandma.'

'We used to have hot cocoa with our lunches every noon.' Grandma warmed to her story. 'For one entire year, I was in charge of making the cocoa.' She giggled and put her hand to her mouth. 'But I was caught, and wasn't allowed to do it the next year.'

'Caught doing what?' Binky wondered.

Grandma giggled again. 'I learned that if I left some of the sugar out of the cocoa, no one liked it as much. When everyone had enough, I'd add more sugar and drink the rest myself.'

'Grandma, you sly fox,' Lexi laughed.

'Wasn't I?' Grandma beckoned to Binky and Jennifer. 'Shall I tell you about my friends, Tillie and Esther? We used to have fine times together. Tillie and I would ride horseback. Once, after the circus had been to town, we decided that we could ride standing up just like those circus performers. I got up on the back of my horse and I went quite a way before I fell off.' Grandma giggled, 'Tillie stood up and knocked herself silly when the horse ran under a low-hanging tree branch.' She sighed. 'Those were the days.'

Then Grandma reached out and touched Jennifer's golden hair. 'Do you remember those days, Tillie?' she asked, her brow furrowed. 'We had so much fun, didn't we?'

Jennifer glanced at Lexi in alarm. Lexi took Grandma's arm. 'This isn't Tillie, Grandma. It's my friend, Jennifer, remember?'

'Oh, Tillie, I loved you so much. Why haven't you come to see me?' Grandma asked sadly, tears forming in her eyes.

Calmly, Lexi tried to distract her, 'Grandma, why don't you go into the kitchen now and have a cup of tea? Mum's there now.'

'Tea?' Grandma said vaguely.

Lexi helped her up from her chair. 'My friends and I are going upstairs now. Thank you for your stories.'

'Stories?' Grandmother said blankly. She was getting confused again.

After Lexi had settled her grandmother with her mother in the kitchen, she came back into the living room. Jennifer and Binky were sitting there pale and wide-eyed.

'Does she always just fade in and out like that?' Jennifer asked bluntly.

Lexi was grateful for her friend's straightforward question. 'Her good days are becoming fewer and farther between. I love it when she's clear, though. I like to hear her talk about her childhood and her life with my grandfather.'

'When she gets that way, you just try to distract her?'

'Sometimes. It doesn't always work.' Lexi smiled slightly. 'We learn as we go around here.'

'You've changed, Lexi,' Binky said bluntly.

Lexi had no doubt that was true, but she said, 'Oh? In what way?'

'How you handled your grandmother for one thing.' There was admiration in Binky's voice. 'You were really patient and kind. You'd be a good nurse.'

Lexi laughed out loud. 'There were days when I thought no one would ever say anything like that to me, Binky. Thanks. My family has been attending a support group at the hospital to meet with other families who have Alzheimer's patients living in their homes. It helps to relate to others who understand the problems we're having.'

Jennifer looked guilty. 'I think we owe you an apology, Lexi. I don't think any of your friends have really tried to understand what you've been going through.'

Lexi shook her head. 'I don't expect that of you. It's very difficult.' An image of Todd came into her mind. If only *he* understood how desperately she was trying to cope with the pain of her grandmother's illness! Lexi pushed away the thought.

'Come on, let's go upstairs,' she said finally. 'Tell me what you've been up to. It's been a while since we've really talked.'

'It certainly has,' Jennifer said bluntly. 'You never come to the Hamburger Shack any more.'

'Yeah,' Binky said with a pout. 'It's wrecking everything.'

'What's wrecked?'

'Our gang. You know. It's not the same as it used to be. Jennifer, Egg, Harry and I are usually there. Once in a while Anna Marie stops by or Matt Windsor, but you don't come any more, and Todd is rarely there.'

'Not Todd either?' Lexi asked, surprised.

'He's been . . . busy.' Binky looked cautiously at Lexi from the corner of her eye.

'Doing what?' Lexi wondered. 'Working at his brother Mike's garage?'

'I don't know about that,' Binky said. She and Jennifer exchanged a strange, furtive glance.

'All right, you two. What's going on?' Lexi demanded. 'Stop looking at each other like that. You must have some piece of news that you don't want to tell me.'

Even Jennifer looked guilty. 'It's no big deal, Lexi, really, just a rumour.'

An odd, fluttery feeling vibrated in Lexi's stomach. 'A rumour?' What kind of rumour?'

'Well, we were just wondering if Todd had stopped coming to the Hamburger Shack because he's busy with someone else.'

'Oh?' Lexi forced herself to remain calm and relaxed, 'Who?'

'It's not for sure.' Jennifer put her hands up. 'It's just that we heard at lunch a few days ago that Todd had taken Mary Beth Adamson to the cinema last weekend.'

Lexi looked stunned.

'Mary Beth Adamson!'

Todd was *her* boy-friend – at least he had been. What was he doing taking another girl to the cinema?

~ 7 ~

Todd and Mary Beth? Lexi couldn't get the idea out of her head. She had difficulty taking notes in class. It was harder still to keep her gaze from wandering towards Todd in the classes they shared. Lexi felt a sick knot in the pit of her stomach that would not go away.

After school, Binky caught Lexi at her locker. 'Mind if I walk home with you?' Binky wondered.

'Great,' Lexi said. 'I'd be glad of your company.'

Binky looked at Lexi sympathetically, 'I know what you mean. For some reason, I can't get that –' she hesitated, 'you know – rumour out of my head.'

'About Todd and Mary Beth?' Lexi asked.

They walked out of the school doors together and down the pavement towards Lexi's home.

'Right. It *is* just a rumour though. Frankly,' Binky

said, 'it's probably something Minda started to get your goat.'

Lexi rolled her eyes. She and Minda Hannaford had had a bumpy relationship ever since Lexi moved to Cedar River. 'Why would Minda try to do that?'

'You know Minda. She doesn't really need reasons for things. She just does them and thinks about it later.' Binky kicked at a stone and it skipped down the street.

'Since Todd and I haven't been talking, I suppose it's not my business what he does,' Lexi said sadly.

Binky snorted indignantly. 'That's not true. You're still a couple. You're just having a little . . . glitch . . . in your relationship. That's what Egg calls it.'

'Oh he does, does he?' Lexi turned to Binky, her eyes showing faint amusement. 'You and Egg talk about my problems with Todd often?'

Binky grinned. 'When Egg and I aren't fighting, we talk a lot.'

Lexi was tempted to tell her friend to mind her own business, but she knew that Binky and her brother cared deeply for her and Todd. Lexi didn't have the heart to tell Binky to stay out of it.

Besides, it felt rather nice to have someone care about her feelings. 'Want to come inside for something to eat?' Lexi asked when they reached her house. Binky hesitated. 'Chocolate cake, maybe? I think there's some left.'

'You bet,' Binky rubbed her stomach. 'I'm starved.'

'Hello, girls,' Mrs Leighton greeted them. 'I'm glad you're home, Lexi. The timing is perfect.'

'Why is that, Mum?' Lexi asked as she reached for the cake on the work-top.

'Ben's teacher just called me from school. Apparently I'm on some committee, which is meeting right now. Ben was supposed to give me a note but he forgot. I shouldn't be gone long. Do you mind, Lexi?'

Lexi nodded. She was tired, but knew the break would do her mum good. 'No, it will be fine, Mum.'

Grandmother's upstairs having a nap. She's had a very restless day, so I'm hoping she sleeps until I get back.'

'Mind if I keep Lexi company?' Binky asked casually. 'We'll do our homework together.'

'Of course not, Binky,' Mrs Leighton smiled. 'I've missed seeing you around the house. Welcome back.'

Binky bobbed her head. 'I'm glad to be back.'

Mrs Leighton left the house and the girls spread their books out on the table. Binky's bubbly presence had a good effect on Lexi. The time passed quickly as they did their homework and enjoyed their snack.

Lexi and Binky were almost finished with their work when they heard a scraping sound coming from upstairs.

'What was that?' Binky jumped.

Lexi looked toward the stairs. 'Grandma must be awake and having trouble getting out of bed. I'd better go and help her.'

'Is there anything I can do?' Binky offered.

Just then they heard a loud crash and shattering glass.

'What was that?' Binky dropped her pencil to the floor.

A cold chill gripped Lexi.

Both girls pushed away from the table and dashed for the stairs. Lexi was the first to reach Grandma's room. She grabbed the doorknob but was met with resistance when she tried to turn it.

'Oh, no!' Lexi cried. 'She's locked it.'

'Your mother locked your grandmother in the bedroom?' Binky asked.

'No, Grandmother locked herself in. She's been doing that lately. Dad's talked about taking the doorknobs off the doors. Grandma! Grandma, are you all right?'

A shuffling sound came from inside the room. 'Oh, help me, help me,' she cried faintly.

'Grandma? Did you fall?'

There was no answer.

'What are we going to do, Binky?'

'Go in through the window? Do you have a ladder?'

Lexi shook her head. 'We have to get help. I think she's fallen. I'll just call 999.'

Leaving Binky in the hallway, Lexi dashed to her parent's bedroom and picked up the phone. As she explained the situation to the soothing voice on the other end of the line, Lexi could hear Binky rattling the doorknob to Grandmother's room.

'Mrs Carson? Mrs Carson? Can you hear me?'

There was no reply.

'They're sending help right away,' Lexi said as she returned to the landing. 'They can take the door off if they have too. And the paramedics will take care of grandmother if she's hurt. I called Ben's school too and left a message for Mum.'

Lexi looked anxiously at the closed door, 'I hope they hurry. What if she's bumped her head or something? What if she's lying there bleeding?'

'You can hear her moving once in a while, Lexi,' Binky assured her. 'She's probably trying to get up.'

'I should have checked on her earlier,' Lexi said, 'I would have discovered the door was locked and could have called before this happened.'

'You can't be sure of that,' Binky pointed out. 'Don't blame yourself for everything that happens to your grandmother.'

Lexi sighed. 'I suppose you're right.'

'I hear sirens,' Binky said.

The two dashed downstairs to let the emergency services in.

Suddenly the house was filled with people. Lexi led two men with tools upstairs to remove the bedroom door. Paramedics followed, ready to enter the room as soon as they could.

'Lexi, what's happened?' Lexi turned to face her mother, who'd just arrived. 'I got the message at school.'

'Grandma woke up, Mum. When I heard her, I went to check and she'd locked the door. She must have fallen.'

'Oh, dear.' Mrs Leighton looked suddenly pale and weak.

'The paramedics are in there now.'

Lexi's mother pushed her way into the room. 'Mum, Mum.'

Lexi and Binky stood waiting in the hallway. In a few minutes Grandma was carried by on a stretcher. Lexi reached out and brushed her cheek. 'Grandma? Are you all right?'

There was no response.

'She has a bump on her head, Lexi,' her mother said. 'They think she'll be okay. But considering her age and condition, they're going to check everything out at the hospital.'

'I'm sorry, Mum. I'm so sorry.'

'Lexi, there was nothing you could do,' Mrs Leighton said firmly. 'Don't blame yourself for this. It's one of the risks we face attempting to take care of her at home. I'm going to go along to the hospital. You'd better wait here and tell Dad what happened. Ben's getting a ride home with a friend.'

Lexi nodded helplessly. Every time she thought that things simply couldn't get any worse, they did. Every time she thought she was dealing with what life had given her, there was a new blow. Lexi sank tiredly against the wall.

'Miss?' One of the young men who'd come to remove the door was standing there when Lexi opened her eyes. 'I wasn't eavesdropping, but I couldn't help overhearing. Your grandmother has Alzheimer's?'

Lexi nodded wearily.

'It's probably none of my business,' he said, looking a little embarrassed, 'but my uncle has Alzheimer's. My aunt takes care of him at home. He falls occasionally, too. Maybe you wouldn't mind if I told you what the doctor's told her to do?'

It was odd that a disease that she'd never heard of until recently now seemed to take up every waking moment of her life.

'There are some scatter rugs in that bedroom,' he said, nodding toward Grandmother's room. 'My aunt was told to get rid of all such rugs, fix steps that might be broken or have torn carpeting, and scuff up slippery floors. She was also told to invest in good lighting. Maybe these things would also be of help to your grandmother.' He glanced again at the stairway. 'Stairs are the worst. It's so easy for them to become disorientated and fall on stairways.'

Lexi nodded wearily, 'Thank you for your help. I'll tell my parents.'

The young man gave Lexi a sympathetic look. 'Listen, I know how you feel,' he said, surprising Lexi with his straightforwardness. 'There's nothing in the world quite like caring for an Alzheimer's patient. My family knows.'

Lexi felt a warm blush of gratitude. His concern and compassion helped to take the edge off her guilt.

As if he were reading her mind, the young man added, 'And don't feel guilty about all of this. It isn't your fault. You're doing the best you can. Remember that.'

The best you can. Lexi thought about that for a few moments. The best that she was capable of doing didn't seem nearly good enough these days.

~ 8 ~

Most of her father's 'patients' at the veterinary clinic must have been discharged, Lexi noted as she viewed the empty cages. Only Fritz, a dog of unknown breed, still remained for Lexi to feed.

'Hi, boy, how are you today?'

Fritz wagged his stubby tail so violently that the cage trembled. 'I wouldn't like being in here all alone, either,' Lexi consoled the puppy as she scratched his head.

She set food and water inside Fritz's enclosure before hosing out the other cages. Usually her father's clinic was busy when she came to work after school. Today it was unusually quiet.

Lexi put away the mops and antiseptics and entered the hallway leading to her father's office.

'Lexi, would you come in here, please?' he called to her.

Lexi peeked inside the doorway. Dr Leighton was sitting at his desk in a white coat, his feet propped up on the desk and his hands behind his head.

'No more patients today, Dad?'

'The last one just left. Sit down, Lexi.' He motioned towards a chair.

'What's up, Dad?'

Dr Leighton looked very serious, as though searching for just the right words. 'I have some news for you, Lexi. Your mother and I have made a decision concerning your grandmother.'

'Oh, what's that?'

'We've decided it's time to put her in a nursing home.'

Lexi leaned forward and stared at her father. 'Really?'

'Your mother is becoming increasingly worn out attempting to care for her. Grandma's good moments are fewer and farther between. After her fall we decided that it's just got too difficult to keep her at home.

'We feel as if we've been neglecting you and Ben in order to care for Grandmother. Ben's teachers at the Academy say that Ben's progress has slowed somewhat. They believe it has to do with the stress he's feeling at home.'

'You mean you're sending her to a rest home because of Ben and me? I don't want it to be our fault that Grandma has to go away, Dad.'

'No, no. It's not, Lexi. I didn't mean to make it sound that way. We have to send her to a nursing home because she's too difficult to care for at home any longer. In the past week, your mother and I have had only a few hours of sleep each night. That simply can't go on.'

Lexi sat quietly in her chair as a rush of emotions avalanched over her. There was sadness at the thought that Grandma would be leaving them. She still felt somewhat guilty. Perhaps she could have done more for Grandmother. The emotion that made Lexi most uncomfortable, however, was her sense of relief. It had been a very long time since their home had been normal.

'Lexi? Can you tell me what you're thinking?'

Lexi stared at the floor. Should she take the risk and confide in her father? 'It's really hard to talk about, Dad.'

'Try me. I'm a good listener.'

'I feel sad that Grandma isn't going to live with us any more. I think I should have done more to help her.' Lexi swallowed hard. 'But in an awful sort of way, I'm kind of glad.'

There, it was out in the open. The painful, guilt-ridden fact that Lexi was almost glad that Grandma would be living somewhere else.

Instead of being shocked or dismayed, Jim Leighton nodded, 'I've had the same feeling myself, Lexi. And I've been very uncomfortable about it. We all love your grandmother very much, but our lives have been disrupted for a long time. You mustn't punish yourself for feeling relief that things are going to be as they once were. We've done our best and we've tried our hardest. Now it's time for Grandmother to be in a nursing home. She needs more care than we can give her. We'd like to keep her in Cedar River. That way, we'd be able to visit her every day.'

'I could go after school on the nights that I don't work at the clinic,' Lexi offered happily. 'And on Saturdays and Sundays . . .'

'She'll get plenty of company, Lexi. You don't have to make any promises that might be hard to keep.'

Lexi nodded, recognising the wisdom in her father's words. She'd grown up a lot during the time that her grandmother had lived with them. She knew now that no matter how good her intentions, things did not always work out the way she planned. Lexi was older and wiser than she had been before her grandfather died.

Lexi stood up. 'Dad, if you don't mind, I'd like to go home and talk to Grandma now.'

'Of course, Lexi.'

She hurried to her bike, hardly noticing the beautiful spring weather as she pedalled towards her house.

At home, she found Grandmother rocking silently in her chair. Her gnarled hands were gripping the arms of the rocker and her eyes were fixed on the lamp. She stared straight ahead, without expression.

'Grandma,' Lexi said softly. Her grandmother did not even blink. Lexi moved closer to the chair and sat by the fireplace. Grandma didn't seem to know she was there. 'Grandma, I'd like to talk to you,' Lexi began. She'd become used to talking to her grandmother, even though she often didn't respond. There were things Lexi needed to say to her. She hoped and prayed that somehow, some way, some of her words would pierce the cloud surrounding her grandmother's brain just now.

'I have so many things I'd like to tell you, Grandma,' Lexi began, thinking back to the first days after her grandfather's death, when Grandmother had come to live with them. 'I don't know if you knew it or not, but there was a time when you were first living here and we didn't know you were sick, that I was very embarrassed by your behaviour. I never told you I was sorry, Grandma and I'd like to right now. It was a hard lesson for me to learn, Grandma, not to be embarrassed.'

Lexi took one of Grandmother's gnarled hands in her own and caressed it gently. 'I didn't realise that I had some things to learn about my faith too. I thought I had it all worked out. In fact, I suppose I thought I was pretty smart about faith. I thought I had all the answers. But then, when it came to Grandpa's death and your illness, I didn't know the answers.'

Lexi lifted Grandma's hand and rubbed it against her own cheek. She liked the feel of the dryer skin against her softer skin. 'Todd was the one who showed me that I wasn't as smart as I thought I was. He told me I was a hypocrite. He told me that I talked about faith but I didn't always live it. That really hurt my feelings.

'But, in some ways, he was right. He made me examine what I really believed. He made me ask myself if I was just accepting all the things my parents taught me or if I had a faith of my own.

'I'm really fortunate, Grandma. God has given me

lots of gifts, but the biggest one is faith. After that it was much easier to be patient with you and not to be embarrassed by the things you did that you didn't know.

'I wish you could know Todd, Grandma, he's really great. He liked you, I could tell. He doesn't come over any more because of our misunderstandings. He thought I wasn't being patient enough with you. He treats me like a stranger now,' Lexi continued, wistfully.

'I suppose I confused him with my behaviour. That's not surprising. I was awfully confused myself. I've had to turn it over to God, Grandma. I can't worry about Todd. I just have to hope and pray that God straightens out his thinking about this whole thing just like he did mine.'

Lexi stroked her grandmother's knee. 'Sometimes these things take a long time,' Lexi sighed. 'I'm not very patient though. I'd like Todd back.'

Lexi leaned her head against her grandmother's leg. 'I'll miss you, Grandma, when you leave us. Once Ben told me that he liked having you here no matter what you did. He didn't care if you recognised him or not. He didn't care if you walked around the house in strange clothes or went to bed in the middle of the day. He just liked having you here. At first that was hard for me to understand, but now I do. This house is going to be awfully empty without you.'

Lexi spoke frankly the thoughts in her mind and the feelings in her heart. She'd gone too long without being honest. It felt good to have Grandmother gently stroke her hair as she had when Lexi was a child. Her silent presence was comforting.

'Todd says he wants to be a doctor some day, Grandma,' Lexi continued, her mind meandering across the many topics that filled her head. 'I hope that he can be involved in research that finds a cure for this awful disease you have.'

Impulsively, Lexi picked up her grandmother's hand and kissed the tips of her fingers.

'We're going to come and visit you in the nursing home. You may not remember every visit, but if you can feel deep inside yourself that someone loves you, maybe that will help. I'll pray for you, Grandma. I'll put you in God's hands. His hands are big and strong and they can hold anything.' Lexi laughed lightly. 'I learned that the hard way. He's been holding me for a long time.'

Lexi peered into her grandmother's face, 'Are you getting tired, Grandma? I suppose it seems silly for me to sit here and talk to you knowing you aren't understanding, but –'

Suddenly, to Lexi's amazement, Grandmother reached out and gently caressed Lexi's face. She smiled at her granddaughter with a loving, affectionate gaze. For just a moment, Lexi wondered if her mind was clear again. Then her eyes clouded and she drifted off again, the sweet smile still on her face.

'You *did* understand, didn't you Grandma?' Lexi said, joy springing within her, 'You understood and you accepted my apology. I know you did!'

Grandmother stroked Lexi's hair and was silent.

Suddenly, Lexi knew what it was she had to do. She folded her hands over her grandmother's and bowed her head.

'Dear Father,' she prayed, 'take care of my grandmother. Help her to know that she's loved. When the time comes, take her to be with you in that place where her mind will be clear and her health will be perfect again. Thanks God, for everything. Especially for giving me the best grandparents in the whole world.'

Lexi felt as though a heavy weight had been lifted from her shoulders. God was here, in this room, listening to her prayers. Lexi was sure of it. He was there for her as he had been all along. What her mother had told her so many times was true. God didn't move. He was always there for his children, ready to help them, ready to take their hand. Lexi was the one who had moved away for a while, but now she was back, secure in his love.

Lexi jumped to her feet and gave her grandmother a huge kiss on each cheek. 'Thanks for listening. You were always a great listener.'

Lexi lifted her eyes heavenward. 'You too, God. You're the best listener of all.'

'Lexi?' Marilyn Leighton entered the room. 'Did I hear you talking to someone? Is Grandma clear enough to chat today?'

Lexi smiled fondly at her grandmother. 'Grandma's great. We've been having a good conversation. Kind of one-sided, but great just the same.'

Mrs Leighton smiled at the bright expression in her daughter's eyes. 'You're looking particularly happy.'

'I am, Mum.' She gave her mother a kiss. 'Everything's going to be all right.'

Lexi grinned and thrust her fist in the air. 'I feel it in my bones!'

~ 9 ~

'My, oh, my, what a wonderful day,' Lexi hummed, as she stuffed her books into the bottom of her locker at school. Jennifer and Binky exchanged wondering glances at the obvious and surprising change in their friend.

'What's up with you?' Jennifer asked bluntly. 'Singing, humming, smiling. We haven't seen much of that for a while.'

A ripple of happy laughter burst from Lexi. 'I feel great today, that's all. Can't a person sing when the sky is blue and cloudless, and we didn't have a pop quiz in maths after all?'

'Well, certainly. I'd burst into a little tune myself if my history test were cancelled.'

Jennifer put her hand on Lexi's locker and forced Lexi to turn to her, 'We're just trying to say that we're noticing a change in you, Lexi. A *good* change.'

'It's as if we've got the old Lexi back,' Binky said, brimming with enthusiasm. 'You haven't been so happy since . . . before your Grandfather died.'

A hint of sadness flickered over Lexi's eyes, but she did not allow it to remain. 'I know. I'm sorry. I've been really hard to live with, and I'd like to apologise. You've been super friends – patient and understanding.'

'Hey, that's what friends are for,' Jennifer said with a casual shrug. 'It's like I said before. There's even been a day or two in my life that I haven't been as sweet and darling as usual.'

Binky snorted and Lexi giggled. Jennifer crossed her eyes and stuck out her tongue at them.

'All I can say is that you two are absolutely right,' Lexi admitted. 'The days since my grandfather died have been the worst in my life.' She looked at the floor. 'I've been ashamed of the way I acted. I just couldn't seem to help myself. For a while, I was convinced that Lexi Leighton could handle everything. I learned that I can't. Not alone.' She looked from Jennifer to Binky. 'Not without my friends, and especially not without God.'

'But you've always had God, Lexi,' Binky pointed out, looking a little confused.

Lexi nodded. 'I have and I haven't. He's always worked in my life. But somewhere way in the back of my mind, there was a little corner of me who refused to let go and trust him completely. I always wanted to stay in charge. When Grandpa died and Grandma got sick, I realised that their problems were something I couldn't be in charge of in any way. I finally had to "Let go and let God," as they say. I had the opportunity to see what God can do if a person really allows him to work in their life.'

Binky scratched her head. 'This is very deep, Lexi. I don't quite understand it all.'

Lexi bit her lip, wondering how to explain to Binky more clearly what had happened to her. Suddenly, an idea came. 'You know the Lord's Prayer, Binky?'

Binky rolled her eyes. 'Of course. Even *my* family's taught me *that* much. "Our Father, who art in heaven, hallowed be thy name, thy kingdom come, thy will be done, on earth as it is in heaven . . ."'

'There!' Lexi stopped her friend. 'That's the part that always hung me up.'

Binky looked blank. 'Huh?'

'"Thy will be done, on earth as it is in heaven." That's the part of the prayer that always worried me.'

'Yes, how?'

'Think about it, Binky,' Lexi reasoned. 'Do you realise what you're saying? "*Thy* will be done." *God's* will be done. You're asking that whatever God wants to be done will be done.'

'What's so bad about that?' Binky wondered.

'What if *his* will for your life and *your* will for your life aren't the same?'

'You mean, what if God wants something for you that's not in your plans at all?'

'Exactly. Whenever I prayed the Lord's Prayer, I always got just a little hung up on that line, "Thy will be done." I wished I could say, "Your will be done, Lord, as long as it agrees with mine!"'

'I see what you're getting at,' Jennifer said.

'Somewhere inside me, there was this little voice saying, "Don't let him take absolute control, Lexi. He might mess things up for you."' Lexi smiled halfheartedly, 'I didn't realise what was happening until now. Finally that voice is quiet.'

'How did you get it to shut up?' Jennifer asked in her usual blunt and forthright manner.

'I realised that whatever God's will is for me, it's better than whatever I could plan for myself.'

'That's a little strange you know,' Binky said frankly. "Cause I can plan some pretty terrific things for myself.'

'But God's thoughts are much grander and much more generous than we even have a mind to imagine,' Lexi said.

'I don't know about that,' Jennifer interjected. 'I can imagine pretty well.'

'That's true,' Lexi said with a laugh. 'And I can, too. But it's a little like how our parents relate to us. They're looking at the big picture while we're only seeing the events right before our noses. Like your history test, for example. All you want to do is pass it, right?'

'You bet,' Binky rolled her eyes heavenward. 'That's the best plan I've heard all day.'

'Exactly. But it's your plan. And why do you want to pass it?'

Binky gave Lexi a disgusted look. 'So I don't get a

bad grade on my report card, and don't get into trouble at home.'

'And why would you get into trouble at home?'

Binky threw her hands in the air. 'Because we don't have any extra money at our house. My parents want me to get a scholarship so that I can go to a good school.'

'Right!' Lexi crowed. 'Your greatest concern is not getting into trouble at home. Your parents see the big picture. They're seeing you at a good college, becoming a success in life. That's what they want for you. Don't you see? Their plans are much greater for you than simply passing one silly test.'

'Well, I suppose if you look at it that way . . .'

'Well, that's how God sees things. He isn't looking at our lives just for the moment, but our *whole* lives, from beginning to end. He wants things for us that will improve our whole life, not just the moment that we're living in right now.'

Binky whistled. 'That's deep, very deep.'

Jennifer nudged Binky, 'Maybe we shouldn't comment the next time she's in a good mood. I didn't anticipate getting into a conversation like this.'

Lexi laughed. 'Sorry. I'm just feeling so great today. I can't help it.'

Jennifer gave Binky an appraising glance. 'What do you think? Did we like her better grumpy?'

Binky crossed her arms over her slim figure and studied Lexi theatrically. Finally she began to shake her head. 'No, I think I like the happy Lexi better than the gloomy Gus she was.'

Lexi laughed with her teasing friends. She understood how they could be confused by the radical change in her personality. Even Lexi couldn't explain the light, bubbly feeling she had inside. It was as though God had taken away all the heaviness and bitterness that had been weighing her down for so many weeks.

Things had not actually changed so much. Grandfather was still gone. Grandmother was still ill. What *had* changed was Lexi's acceptance of those facts. She'd come to terms with her grandmother's illness. God had given her the opportunity to say what she'd wanted to say to her grandmother. Even through her grandmother's confusion, she'd understood the message of love that Lexi had given her. Grandma was God's responsibility now. He would see her through this troubled time. He would see her whole family through it.

Lexi attended her morning classes with a lightness she hadn't felt for ages. When the noon bell rang, she realised how hungry she was, and hurried to the lunchroom. On the way, she passed Egg's locker. He was busy jamming a sports bag into the already overflowing space. 'Egg,' she greeted him.

He spun around and his serious face split into a huge smile, 'Lexi, hi!'

Impulsively, Lexi threw her arms around him. 'It's good to see you, Egg. You're never going to get that locker closed.' She'd caught him off guard. Egg staggered backwards against the locker, trying to catch his balance.

Lexi giggled as Egg burst into laughter. Then Lexi realised that Todd was standing behind them, his mouth gaping in amazement at the little exchange. Without comment, she placed her index finger on Todd's jaw and closed his mouth for him.

'Great day, isn't it?' she said cheerfully, and turned in the direction of the lunch-room.

Jennifer, Harry Cramer, Binky and Anna Marie were already sitting at the table when Lexi arrived with her dinner tray. 'Hi! What's up?' she greeted them.

Four faces creased into smiles at her cheerful greeting. Lexi felt a twinge of guilt as she noticed the relief in their voices and in their behaviour. She hadn't realised until now how deeply her depression had run or how much it had affected her friends.

She knew it had been very awkward since she and Todd had had their disagreement. Lexi was determined not to put her friends through anything like that again.

When Egg and Todd arrived at the lunch table, everyone was telling jokes and laughing.

Egg started in on his usual 'knock-knock' jokes, and when Harry realised none of them were new, he began to pile empty milk cartons and napkins on to his tray. 'I've got to go. Frankly, if I listen to one more of Egg's sick jokes, my mind will be ruined. It will be total mush. All capability for logical thought will be lost.'

'Are you trying to tell me you don't like my jokes, Harry?' Egg asked indignantly.

'Whatever gave you that idea?'

'Well, I have to go to my locker and pick up my

books,' Binky said, leaving with Harry. 'I've built up a pretty good tolerance for Egg's jokes, and even *I've* had enough.'

Egg took the playful teasing well. 'Just you wait. I'll get even. I found a great new joke book in the library the other day. In fact there's a whole section on knock-knock jokes. Listen to this one –'

Five voices chimed in together, 'Go away, Egg. We don't want any!'

As the others trooped away, Lexi remained. When she turned around, Todd was standing behind her, watching.

'Oh,' she said, surprised. 'I thought you'd gone.'

'Not yet,' he said. 'There's something I want to tell you.'

Lexi felt a flutter in her stomach. *Todd. It's been so long.*

His blue eyes were sharp, almost piercing. 'Welcome back, Lexi,' he said softly. 'I've missed you.'

It was an awkward moment. But Lexi knew exactly what he meant. Her old self, her real self, had been lost for a while. She had been sunk into a pit of grief, pain and confusion. It had changed her. Even more than she realised. But God had brought her through all the bitterness and pain. She was stronger now, wiser and more compassionate than before.

Lexi stared back at Todd. His golden blonde hair was softly feathered away from his face. His broad shoulders and sturdy frame seemed fixed and unmoving. His deep blue eyes were appraising her. It was the 'new and improved' version he was seeing, even though

Lexi was at a loss for speaking of it.

She had hurt and confused him. Because of her unusual behaviour he had become wary of her. There was so much she wanted to say, to explain. So many feelings, so many emotions, and so few words seemed to fit to express them. It had been a shattering lesson to Lexi to learn how weak she really was.

She didn't have all the answers any more. It had taken all the problems at home to bring her to the place of realising this, of realising that she had to depend upon God alone.

In the noise and clatter of the lunch-room, she couldn't bring herself to speak, hoping that another opportunity would present itself for her to explain her new feelings. So she simply smiled.

'I'm glad to see you smiling again,' Todd said.

Lexi bowed her head slightly. 'I'm glad to *be* smiling, Todd. It's been a long time.'

He hesitated, then turned to head for the door. 'I'll see you later, Lexi.'

'Okay,' she answered wistfully. Taking her tray to the counter, Lexi ran into Minda Hannaford.

She was wearing one of her more up-to-date outfits – a short, tight, blue suede skirt, a bright yellow, off-the-shoulder top, and a wide black belt. Her earrings were huge, almost touching her shoulders. Minda's hair was pulled into a ponytail on the left side of her head, and her fringe was spiked in every direction.

Lexi managed to smile broadly at her. 'Hello, Minda. How are you?'

'Oh, hi,' Minda responded, casting a suspicious glance at Lexi.

'I really liked your article on fashion in the latest *River Review*,' Lexi said honestly. 'You definitely have a feel for it.'

Minda's eyes lit up. 'Thanks. I notice a lot of the girls are wearing more neon colours since I wrote about it,' she said, looking a little smug.

'You're really sharp. Keep up the good work, Minda.'

Minda's eyes narrowed. 'What are you so cheerful about today?'

Apparently even Minda had noticed Lexi's depression lately.

'Well, I've been down for a long time, but I'm feeling much better now.'

'I didn't know people like you could get depressed. You've always been so bright, cheerful and . . . perky.' Minda looked Lexi up and down. 'I thought you were stuck on perky.'

'Really?' Lexi asked, looking serious.

'Don't get bent out of shape over it. It's just that I thought that perpetual smile of yours was glued to your face.'

'Well, life hasn't been smooth for me for the last while, but things are starting to turn around.' Lexi wondered why she was saying all this to Minda.

'I didn't realise things ever went wrong in your life. Except how your brother is . . . you know.'

'My grandfather passed away,' Lexi blurted.

'Oh, I'm sorry, I didn't know that.' Minda's expression changed.

'That's okay. I didn't say much about it. Then my grandmother came to live with us.'

'Really?' Minda made a face. 'That must be a drag.'

'More than you know. Grandma has Alzheimer's disease.'

Minda's dark eyebrows arched. 'Alzheimer's? Wow, that's heavy. I did a report on that last year for Science class.' Her expression was almost compassionate. 'I read a bunch of books and magazine articles on it. I know it must be awful, especially how it affects the family. It even made me cry to read about it.'

Lexi was seeing a new side of Minda Hannaford.

'They do bizarre things, don't they?'

Lexi nodded. 'Yes. My grandmother is deteriorating quickly now. She's silent most of the time. She can't seem to find words to express herself any more.' As strange as it seemed to be telling this to Minda, Lexi felt compelled to continue.

'For a long time, we didn't know what was wrong with my grandmother. Once she came downstairs with her underwear on the outside of her clothing, and another time she wore high heels with her dressing gown. Our greatest fear was that she would burn herself or hurt herself in some other way. Now, she just sits most of the day in her rocker and remains quiet. But we can't be sure when she will wander off or become disorientated.'

'She still lives with you, then?' Minda asked.

'Yes, but not for long. My parents are arranging to put her into a nursing home. It's getting too hard for my mother to care for her. Sometimes Grandma doesn't sleep at night, and she keeps Mum up.'

'That's interesting. My research showed that the families of Alzheimer's patients are the real victims. They get trapped caring for people who don't even realise who they are or what is being done for them. One of the magazine articles mentioned day care centres. I wonder if Cedar River has one?'

'I wish it did,' Lexi answered. 'There is a support group for families at the hospital. It's the closest thing we've found.'

Minda shifted her weight nervously. 'Well, I'm sorry. About your grandfather, and your grandmother and all. I guess I didn't realise you were having a bad time. That must mean that things go wrong even in perfect people's lives.'

Lexi smiled faintly. 'I'm not perfect, Minda. Far from it. In the past few weeks, I've been reminded of it over and over again.'

'Hey, Minda,' someone called from across the cafeteria. 'Are you coming, or not?'

Minda glanced in their direction.' Yes, I'll be right there.' She looked at Lexi again. 'Well, I really am sorry about everything.' She paused then, and Lexi could tell she was thinking deeply. 'Maybe there's something else I should mention.'

'Yes?'

'There was a rumour going around school that Todd had taken Mary Beth to a film.'

Lexi's eyes widened. 'Yes, I know. I heard.'

'It wasn't true,' Minda said bluntly. 'Actually, they

ran into each other there and sat a couple of rows apart. I expect someone saw them coming out of the theatre at the same time and thought . . . you know.'

Lexi nodded, wondering why Minda was telling her this.

Then the question was answered for her. 'I just thought you might like to know that, since you've had such a hard time at home and all . . . One less thing to worry about, right?'

'Right.'

Minda strutted away then, towards her friend. She held her head high and looked tough and self-assured.

Lexi smiled to herself as she finally placed her tray on the counter and left the lunch-room. Minda had really been nice to her. And the one issue that had really been bothering Lexi was settled. God *did* work in mysterious ways!

~ *10* ~

The day finally came.

Lexi glanced out of the bedroom window at the bright blue sky. An occasional puffy white cloud scudded across it. The sun was warm and bright. Nature, at least, seemed at peace with itself. Today was the day the Leightons were to take Grandma Carson to the nursing home.

Lexi, knowing how difficult it would be for her mother, had volunteered to help Grandma Carson pack her suitcase. Though Grandma was confused, she seemed to know what was going on around her. A few tears rolled down her soft, wrinkled cheek.

'Look, Grandma, we'll put all your pretty night-dresses in this suitcase,' Lexi said, trying to remain cheerful. 'When we get to your new room, we'll unpack them and put them in a drawer, so you'll know exactly where they are.'

It was awful. Lexi felt like a traitor.

'How are you doing, Lexi?' Mr Leighton entered the room and surveyed the clutter of suitcases and clothing. Then he noticed his mother-in-law crying quietly.

'I'm almost ready, Dad. If I've forgotten anything, we can run it over later.'

Mr Leighton nodded. 'You're being a big help to your mother, Lexi. She's lying down right now.'

'She's taking this pretty hard, isn't she?'

'Understandably so. She thought she could manage. Now she's feeling that she's failed.'

'But she didn't fail, Dad. Grandma's had a lot of good times here. It's just that now –' Lexi's voice trailed away as she looked at her grandmother.

'You're right, Lexi,' Mr Leighton said softly. 'But she's declining quickly. It just doesn't work to keep her here.'

Lexi nodded, her lips pressed together in a tight line. The worse thing that had developed lately was that Grandmother seemed to have forgotten how to care for her own body.

Lexi had always taken for granted that once a person learned how to dress, brush her teeth, and eat properly, she would never forget. But the illness had caused her grandmother to forget some of those simple behavioural patterns. She needed to be shown how to brush her teeth and feed herself.

Lexi had expected the procedure to bother her. Oddly enough it hadn't. Lexi viewed helping her grandma as an opportunity to show her with both actions and words that she loved and cared for her.

Mrs Leighton set out clean clothes for Grandma Carson every morning and carried away the soiled ones from the day before, otherwise Grandmother would put the dirty clothes on again, not able to distinguish between them. Some days, she couldn't dress herself at all.

She also refused to take a bath. Even though Grandma Carson had always believed that cleanliness was virtue, it now took as long as an hour to coax her into the water.

Still, Mrs Leighton insisted that her mother look as nice as possible, even though Grandma herself was beyond caring. She would carefully help her put on a small amount of make-up, just enough to brighten her pale cheeks and faded lips. And her hair was kept clean and shiny and neatly in place.

Lexi closed the last suitcase. 'There, Grandma, we're all set. I'll tell Dad to come and get the suitcases and take them to the car.'

'I don't want to go.'

Lexi glanced up startled, as Grandma rarely spoke these days. 'What did you say?'

Grandma Carson stared straight ahead as if she hadn't said anything. *She knows*, Lexi thought to herself. *She knows that she's going to be leaving here and she doesn't want to go.* Tears sprang into Lexi's eyes.

Why does it have to be so hard, God? There was no bitterness or anger in her question. *Please, help her through this, God. Help us all.*

Just then, Mr Leighton entered the room. 'The car's ready, Lexi. I'll carry these suitcases down. Your mother will come to help you get Grandmother down the stairs.'

They took the stairs one at a time. Grandmother had not been eating well and her body was frail and thin.

Ben stood by the door with tears dripping down his cheeks. 'I don't want Grandma to go,' he wailed. 'She's my friend.'

'Grandma's my friend, too,' Lexi pointed out to Ben. 'But we can't take care of her any more, pet. What if Grandma fell here and hurt herself?'

'Ben would watch her. Ben would watch her really closely.'

'I'm sorry, Ben. That's too big a responsibility for you. You have to go to school at the Academy. Wouldn't it be much easier if after school we went to visit Grandmother at the nursing home?'

'Every day?' Ben asked.

'Often,' Lexi promised.

As they drove towards the nursing home, Lexi noticed that Grandma's confusion seemed to clear. She looked around her with interest as they pulled into the driveway.

While Mr Leighton unloaded the suitcases and Mrs Leighton talked to the administrator in the office, Lexi took her grandmother by the arm, 'Grandma, I have some friends here that I'd like you to meet.'

'Friends?'

'Yes. Todd and I used to come here and bring

fudge. I have lots of friends here – some very nice people. Come on.' Lexi led Grandma down the hall. They stopped in front of an old man strapped in a wheelchair. 'Mr Norris,' Lexi said, speaking as loudly as she dared, knowing the old man was very deaf, 'Mr Norris.'

He looked up from beneath his bushy, grey eyebrows. 'Lexi? Did you bring me some fudge?'

Lexi laughed. 'Not today, Mr Norris, but I have someone I want you to meet.'

Mr Norris eyed Grandma speculatively. 'Who is this pretty young thing?'

'This is my grandmother, Mr Norris. She's going to be living here now.'

Mr Norris's smile widened, 'Well, well, isn't that wonderful news? That means you'll be coming to see us more often.'

Lexi laughed and shook a finger at the old man. 'You just want more fudge. I know you.'

Mr Norris grinned, but didn't deny the accusation. As they walked down the hall, Lexi introduced each of the elderly people that she knew to her grandmother. Though she was quiet, Lexi could feel her grandmother's body relaxing as they walked.

'You can see, Grandma, that I have lots of friends here. I'll be coming to visit you as often as I can. It might seem very strange and different now, but it's going to be all right. The people here are nice. They really are.'

'I think this is going to be your room, Grandma. Shall we take a look at it?'

They walked into a sun-filled room painted in a bright yellow. There were fresh white curtains at the window and a big yellow easy chair in one corner. Another elderly woman sat in a straight-backed chair, knitting industriously. A brass and wicker bird cage hung above her with a small yellow canary inside. The bird chirped cheerfully and flitted from his swing to the side of the cage and back again.

'A bird,' Grandma said.

Lexi detected the delight in her voice. Grandma Carson had always loved birds. She'd fed them year-round at her house in Oxford City. She seemed more delighted to see the bird than to meet her room-mate. While her parents were getting her grandmother settled, Lexi walked out into the hall. Tears formed and threatened to fall. She didn't want her grandmother or her parents to see her crying now.

Lexi paced the hall, her head down, her eyes fixed on the toes of her shoes. She nearly lost her breath when she ran smack into the hard wall of Todd Winston's chest.

'Todd! What are you doing here?'

He held out a box of foil-wrapped packages. 'We're delivering fudge. Mum offered to help me make it.'

'But, you and I do that.'

'It's been a long time, Lexi.' Todd shrugged. 'You haven't been around.' He paused thoughtfully. 'I didn't know you wanted to do it any more.'

'Frankly, I've missed doing it,' Lexi admitted.

Todd looked surprised.

Just then, Mrs Winston joined them. 'This is great

fun,' she said. 'These old people are just wonderful. They have so many stories to tell.' She took the box of fudge from Todd. 'Why don't you let me finish these deliveries? It's such a marvellous excuse to start a conversation. How are you, Lexi?' Mrs Winston smiled. 'I haven't seen you for a while.'

'I haven't been around much. We're checking my grandmother into the rest home today.'

'That must be very difficult.'

Lexi sighed. 'It is. I didn't realise how difficult it could be.'

'Well, this is a good home, Lexi,' Mrs Winston assured her. 'They'll take good care of your grandmother here.'

'What am I supposed to do now that you've taken over my job?' Todd asked his mother, with a smug grin.

Mrs Winston shrugged. 'Well, Lexi looks a little lost. Why don't you do something together. I imagine you have some catching up to do.' Her eyes twinkled. 'Go on. Why don't you have lunch at the Hamburger Shack? That way I won't have to cook when I get home.'

Lexi glanced at Todd out of the corner of her eye, curious about his reaction to his mother's suggestion.

'We could do that,' Todd said without conviction. He looked at Lexi. 'What do you think?'

'Sounds good to me. It's been a long, sad day for me so far.'

'See you later,' Mrs Winston chirped. 'I've got people to see and fudge to deliver.'

112

Todd and Lexi stood there for a long moment in awkward silence, as if neither knew what to say or do. How different it was from when they were so comfortable around one another!

Lexi finally found her tongue. 'I'd better tell my parents where we're going.'

Todd nodded and followed her towards her grandmother's room.

They found her sitting in her rocking chair singing softly. Her eyes were closed, and the sun filtered across her face in warm reflection. Lexi paused in the doorway, surprised and a bit startled. Grandmother looked so young, so peaceful.

'She looks comfortable, doesn't she?' Mrs Leighton enthused. 'Hello, Todd. Nice to see you.'

'Thank you Mrs Leighton.'

'I think it's the canary,' Mrs Leighton went on with a chuckle. 'As soon as she saw it, she felt at home. Her birthday's coming up. Maybe we could get her a pair of songbirds.'

'Since Grandma's so comfortable, do you mind if I leave, Mum?' Lexi asked. 'Todd's mother suggested we get lunch at the Hamburger Shack.'

Mr Leighton, quiet until now, pulled out his wallet and handed Todd a ten-dollar bill. 'Sounds like a great idea. And while Ben is at his friend's house, I think I'll take your mother out for a leisurely lunch. It's been a while.' He smiled, and the months of worry and weariness seemed to be erased from his face.

'I think that's a wonderful idea, Dad. I'll see you two later. Thanks.'

'Thank you, Mr Leighton,' Todd added. 'See you soon.'

As they left the room and walked down the corridor, Todd commented, 'Your grandmother did look very content.'

Lexi smiled. 'It's going to be all right. I just know it is. I've prayed a lot about this day. I think it's the best decision we could make for Grandma.' She sighed. 'At first, I wondered if putting her in a nursing home meant we'd failed. Now, I don't feel that way at all. It just means that now is the time for something new.'

Todd looked thoughtful, and then he began quoting a passage of scripture, '*For everything there is a season and a time for every matter under heaven.*'

'Ecclesiastes,' Lexi said with a smile. 'I had to learn those verses for a Sunday school class when I still lived in Grover's Point. The passage fits, doesn't it?'

They paused in the lobby of the nursing home. On a table of books and magazines, Lexi spotted a Gideon Bible. She picked it up and opened it to Ecclesiastes chapter 3. Todd moved in closer, and together they read the words.

A time to be born and a time to die, a time to plant and a time to uproot, a time to kill and a time to heal, a time to tear down and a time to build, a time to weep and a time to laugh, a time to mourn and a time to dance, a time to scatter stones and a time to gather them, a time to embrace and a time to refrain, a time to search and a time to give up, a time to keep and a time to throw away, a time to tear and a time to mend, a time to be silent and a time to speak, a time to love and a time to hate, a time for war and a time for peace . . . He has made everything beautiful in its time. He has also set eternity in the hearts of men; yet they cannot fathom what God has done from beginning to end.

'Amazing, isn't it?' Lexi said softly. 'For every situation in a person's life, for everything that happens, there seems to be something in the Bible that relates to it.'

'Very true,' Todd said with a smile.

Lexi closed the Bible and laid it on the table. There *was* a time for everything. She thought of Grandma's contented expression as she sat in the rocker with the sun filtering across her face, and the tiny yellow bird singing in its cage. It was so good too, to see her own mother so happy and at peace. She would cling to the image.

~ 11 ~

It felt both odd and wonderful to climb into Todd's old car. The navy blue '49 Ford Coupe was as shiny as a new penny. Lexi leaned against the velvety upholstery and sighed. She'd missed this more than she'd realised.

Todd and Lexi were quiet as they drove through the streets of Cedar River towards the Hamburger Shack. But the silence was not hostile as it had been before. Lexi was content. It didn't seem necessary to say anything.

The car-park was nearly empty, and once inside they noticed only three tables were in use. Lexi and Todd automatically walked to the back of the cafe, to the alcove they had shared so often.

Jerry Randall greeted them from the counter. 'Hi, there! Long time no see.'

Jerry was the first boy Lexi'd met when she moved to Cedar River. That seemed like a hundred years ago. She sank into the alcove with a sigh.

'What do you want for lunch?' Todd asked.

Lexi shrugged. 'The usual. I'm starving.' For the first time in weeks she didn't feel a nervous fluttering in her stomach.

'Hamburgers, chips, and milk then?'

'Sounds fine to me.'

Todd placed the order with Jerry, then as he turned away, Todd called him back, 'You'd better add a banana split to that. Bring two spoons.'

After some small talk, the food arrived and they quietly devoured their hamburgers.

Lexi picked at the last of her chips, and looked up meekly at Todd, 'I have something I'd like to say, Todd.' Her voice quivered a little.

'Okay. Fire away.'

'I – I'd like to apologise for confusing you. For creating the misunderstandings that we had. I'm sorry for my actions that caused our disagreement.'

Todd had a faintly sad look in his eyes. 'I have some things I'm sorry for too, Lexi.'

'Okay. But let me say what I'm thinking first. I know that you didn't understand how I could talk about faith in God and acceptance of people as they are, and then not seem to accept the fact that my grandfather had died and my grandmother was ill.'

Todd opened his mouth to speak, but Lexi went on. It was difficult enough to get this out, without interruptions.

'When you told me you thought I was a hypocrite, I was hurt, insulted and angry. I thought it was one of the cruellest things you could say to me, Todd, because I'd been *priding* myself on being such a good Christian,' Lexi sighed. 'Sounds really silly now – proud to be a good Christian. I guess that's what a hypocrite is. You were right. You were perfectly right and I didn't even see it.'

'Lexi, I –'

'But it hurt anyway, Todd. It did some good though. It made me think. For the first time in my whole life, it made me examine what it really meant to be a Christian. I had to think about what I believed. I had to decide whether the Christianity I was spouting was just the lessons my parents had taught me or if Christianity was something I believed for myself.'

'And?' Todd was hanging on every word now.

'The faith I have is mine, Todd. It's not something handed from generation to generation like old silver or china dishes. And my faith is stronger than ever. Not because of anything I did but because of what God did for me. He gives us everything, Todd. He even gives us the faith we need in order to believe in him.'

'I'm glad for you, Lexi,' he said softly.

She smiled, relieved that she'd said what she'd wanted to say for so long. 'You were pretty brave Todd, telling me that I was behaving like a hypocrite. I'd really begun to depend on myself. I thought I was strong. God had almost become secondary in solving my problems. It was easy to preach about God to others. It was a lot harder to let him take over completely in my own life. It took this whole experience to make me realise that God is the only one who can get people through bad times.'

'I didn't mean to hurt you, Lexi. I really didn't.' Lexi could see the pain in Todd's dark eyes.

'I deserved it,' Lexi said with a short laugh. 'That time anyway.'

Todd wrinkled his brow. 'What time do you mean?'

'The time you called me a hypocrite. The other time, I didn't deserve it at all.'

Todd's expression clouded. 'I don't understand.'

'Do you remember the day you came to see me and I sent my grandmother to her room for a nap?'

'Oh.' Todd's face darkened. 'Yes.'

'You accused me of being impatient and treating my grandmother like a child. I could tell you were upset and frustrated. I understand now that you were probably more upset because of the way my grandmother was behaving. Alzheimer's is an ugly disease, Todd. It's terrible to watch it happen to someone you love. You have to treat them like a child, because in their mind, that's what they are.'

Todd nodded, ashamed of his lack of understanding. 'I know that now, Lexi. I've been doing a lot of reading in the school library about Alzheimer's disease. I know and understand more now than I did at the time. I think my pride stood in the way too. I should have come back and apologised – told you I was wrong, but I was confused.' He looked embarrassed. 'I suppose that means we're both real honest-to-goodness people, flaws and all, huh?'

119

'You're right about that. We had to learn it the hard way, didn't we?'

He reached across the table and took Lexi's hands in his. 'I can't tell you how much I've missed you, Lexi. I hated every day at school when I saw you and couldn't talk to you. I was ashamed of myself for being so critical when I really didn't understand your situation. Then I was embarrassed and didn't know what to do any more. I felt like I'd created some big mess that I'd never find my way out of.'

'Oh, Todd –'

'I think these have been the worst days of my whole life,' he admitted. 'I missed not talking to you on the telephone at night and eating lunch with you during the day. The whole gang was mad at me. They told me I should "shape up and make up" with you 'cause we'd wrecked all their fun.'

'They did?' Lexi said, a huge smile breaking across her face. 'They never told *me* that.'

Todd looked sheepish. 'They blamed me for all our trouble. They were more understanding about your grandmother's illness than I was. I should have been the one who was there for you, Lexi. Instead, I caused you *more* trouble.' He smiled weakly. 'I've paid the price, though. Every day seemed more empty than the day before, without you around. I got a huge cheque from my brother Mike because I worked about three times more than usual. I didn't have anything else to do!' Todd squirmed in his seat. 'I even thought maybe I could get you out of my mind if I talked to other girls. But it wasn't the same. There's no one like you.'

'Not even Mary Beth Adamson?' Lexi said cautiously.

Todd jerked his head up and a blush seeped up his neck and across his cheeks. 'I didn't ask her out, Lexi. I know that's the rumour going around school, but I didn't. I wished someone would tell you –'

'Someone did,' Lexi said. 'Minda.'

Todd's eyes widened in surprise. 'Minda?' he echoed.

'I expect she felt sorry for me,' Lexi said with a smile. 'Even Minda has a heart.'

'It's bigger than I thought it was,' Todd said with a grin. 'I think I'll thank her the next time I see her.' He paused. 'Do you know what I discovered during the time we were apart?'

Lexi shook her head, anxious to hear what he would say next.

'There is something very special and unique about you. I don't know what it is, but I felt it the first time I met you. You're one of a kind – my kind.' 'Oh, Todd –' Lexi felt the warmth in her face. *That's the nicest thing you've ever said to me, Todd Winston*, she thought to herself.

'I also wanted you to know that I have been praying for you, Lexi. For you *and* your grandmother.'

Lexi nodded knowingly. 'I could feel it.'

'You could?' Todd blurted.

As Todd squeezed her hands across the table, Lexi felt as though her heart would burst with happiness. She wanted this moment to last forever.

But it was not to be.

There was a commotion at the entrance of the restaurant. Egg, Binky, Jennifer and Harry came bursting into the room laughing and talking loudly. They headed for their usual table, Egg doing one of his exotic bird routines. He waddled like a penguin, his heels together, his feet splayed outward, his hands flapping at his sides.

He stopped short when he spied Todd and Lexi holding hands in 'their' alcove. 'Do my eyes deceive me?' he said, giving a low whistle. 'Look who we have here!'

The others spotted the twosome at the same time. 'All right!' Binky shouted, punching the air with her fist. Harry stuck his fingers between his teeth and gave a shrill whistle, and Jennifer gave a gusty cheer, 'Yes!'

'Do you think they're happy to see us?' Todd asked Lexi with a twinkle in his eye.

'I certainly hope so. I'd hate to see this much weird behaviour for nothing.'

'Does this scene mean what I think it means?' Jennifer asked as she slid in next to Lexi.

'Well, I suppose that depends on what you think it means,' Todd said, looking amused.

'They're back together!' Binky squealed, jumping around in little circles.

'This calls for a celebration,' Egg announced. 'Chocolate shakes and onion rings – *on me*.'

'Egg McNaughton, you don't have any money,' Binky reminded him.

'Oh, yeah. Iced water and napkins on me,' he announced sheepishly, refusing to have his good mood squelched.

'Maybe I should be the one to treat everyone,' Todd

said with a broad grin. 'After all, I must be the happiest man in town today. Ice cream for everybody – on me.'

The announcement sent everyone rushing to the counter, before he could withdraw his offer.

'I'll take a triple dip. Chocolate, strawberry cheese-cake and pineapple yogurt,' Binky blurted to Jerry Randall, who stood behind the counter amused as anyone.

'That's disgusting!' Egg remarked as he pushed up beside his sister. 'I'll have a triple dip of bubble gum, liquorice and peppermint candy.'

'Now, *that's* disgusting.'

As the two argued about who made the better choice, the others burst into laughter.

Lexi felt warm and secure across from Todd, as he kept her hands in his. Nothing else mattered. It was one of the most wonderful times of her life, coming after such a long, bleak period.

But it wasn't just Todd and their friends – it was more than that. Lexi felt a deep river of peace in her whole being. She had a strong faith and new strength that had not been hers before in quite the same way.

She felt she could handle whatever became of her grandmother now. She could cope with events in her own life. There was a sure confidence that God was on her side. He would not leave her alone. He had told her that in his word. God had promised to support her and love her forever, and he didn't break promises. She knew now that all she had to do was to depend on him instead of upon herself.

Lexi was pulled from her thoughts by the sound of Egg eating his cone next to her. 'This *is* pretty gross,' he admitted – pink, black and green ice cream dripping down his arm. 'I probably should have left out the liquorice.'

At his bewildered look, Lexi burst into gales of laughter. She flung her arms around Egg's neck and impulsively kissed him on the cheek. 'I love you, Egg NcNaughton.'

Startled by the outburst, Egg tipped his cone sideways and all three scoops fell in a heap on the table. He shook his head and grinned at Lexi. 'We're really glad you're back. We missed you.'

Lexi felt a bubble of joy rise within her. 'I've got the best friends –' she looked shyly at Todd, 'and the best boy-friend in the whole world. Thanks, everybody. Thanks a lot!'

This story is set in the USA where there are hospital support groups. In the UK The Alzheimer's Disease Society have a network of support groups throughout the country who can offer help, advice and support.
For further information contact:

The Alzheimer's Disease Society
158–160 Balham High Road
London SW12 9BN
Tel. 081 675 6557

Some more books in the *Impressions* series
Hidden Prizes
Audrey Constant
Paula is starting a promising career in show jumping. But there are rival priorities. Her family need her help on the farm and she wants to organise riding lessons for disabled children.

Paula has to make some difficult decisions and she discovers that rewards are not always what you expect.

Penguin Theatre
Veronica Heley
Sam is on a trip of a lifetime to see penguins in Antarctica. Flashbacks show her struggle with dyslexia, her love of backstage theatre work and the events leading to the exciting trip. Through Sam's diary we discover the awe-inspiring world of the Antarctic.

For the Love of Money
Trevor Roff
Baz and Nick raid the council office safe and at first congratulate themselves on a successful job. But their getaway has been seen by Nick's brother, Damian, who is torn between loyalty for his brother and guilt at an innocent man being accused of the crime. The suspect is a member of the beach mission team and tension rises as he is arrested.

Love and Laura
Audrey Hopkins

A writing assignment for the summer holidays? Laura jumps at the chance because she wants to be a writer. She chooses love as her subject and remembers the times in her life when love has been all important.

Then she meets David and through their friendship the project merges with what is happening now.

Walking Disaster
Gail Vinall

Mel is stunned when she is not selected for the school team for the annual Ten Tors hike. She cannot believe that the reason is because she lacks team spirit.

Mel joins the church youth club instead, feeling she is doing them a favour but on the hike she is in for some surprises.

Rat Pack
Mollie Thompson

Gail and her Rat Pack are well known for their bullying tactics. When Rachel stands up for herself Gail is so furious that she plans her revenge with no thought for the consequences. She discovers that followers can be fickle as the Rat Pack melts away.